UNDER THE GULF COAST SUN

UNDER THE GULF COAST SUN

SKIP RHUDY

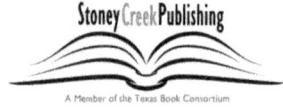

Published by

Stoney Creek Publishing Group

StoneyCreekPublishing.com

Copyright © 2025 by Skip Rhudy. All rights reserved.

ISBN: 978-1-965766-04-0
ISBN (ebook): 978-1-965766-05-7
Library of Congress Control Number: 2025900384

No part of this book may be reproduced in any form or by any electronic or mechanical means, including information storage and retrieval systems, without written permission from the author, except for the use of brief quotations in a book review.

This book is a work of fiction. Names, characters, places, and incidents are either the product of the author's imagination or are used fictitiously, and any resemblance to actual persons, living or dead, business establishments, events or locales is entirely coincidental.

Cover design by Ken Ellis

Printed in the United States

ONE

CONNOR O'REILLY SQUINTED toward the sun rising over the Texas Gulf, its golden rays fanning around a towering purple thunderhead—*like wings,* he conjured, *like an angel and a promise.*

Something good was coming.

"There might be better waves than we hoped for," he said aloud, noisily sipping coffee that smelled better than it tasted. It burned his lips, and he flinched.

The ever-fickle Gulf, though, did not provide. The early morning waves he and his friend Kevin Stamford had paddled out to—glassy, with good form and increasing in size—degenerated quickly after the thunderclouds vanished.

The waves became a mess, not worth staying in position for, so they drift-surfed, letting the current carry them as far as it wanted, but they eventually got sick of it and paddled in. The onshore wind was so strong that it whipped the boards back and forth under their arms. Connor stopped, put his surfboard on his chest, then stuck his belly out. The wind held it in place—no hands.

At first, that made them laugh.

"Damn wind," Stamford said, spitting onto the sand. "It's a washing machine out there."

They got back to Stamford's truck. Connor dumped his board in the back, then grabbed the towel he'd brought and slung it over his shoulders as he got in the passenger side. Disgusted, he slammed the door. Out the front window, he saw a churn of disorganized waves and dirty brown whitewater chop. Sand blew fast across the beach as small birds dashed mindlessly from one shoreline puddle of vanishing seawater to the next. A moment later, his friend got in the driver's side. Water droplets dripped off Stamford's puka shell necklace as he grabbed his sunglasses hanging from the rearview mirror and slipped them on.

They both sat in silence as wind gusts buffeted the Chevy Luv.

Connor opened the small ice chest between them, extracted a can of Lone Star from the ice, pulled the tab and started guzzling.

"Kassie Hernandez is coming to Port Aransas next week," Stamford said.

Partway through a gulp, Connor spat. White foam shot out against the windshield.

"No way!" Stamford shouted.

He slugged Connor's arm.

"Ow!"

Connor shrank back. Beer foam washed over the dashboard, white dribbles streaming over the radio. Stamford snatched Connor's towel and vigorously wiped the beer off the windshield, dash, and radio, then tossed the towel forcefully to the floorboard. The beer had been wiped up, but its yeasty smell filled the truck.

"Come on, man," said Connor, grabbing his towel and knocking the sand off. "What was that for?"

"You ass," Stamford answered, shaking his head. "I should make you get out and walk back to Port Aransas."

"Totally your fault," Connor said, gesturing with his beer can at the dash. "Besides, how would you know Kassie's coming down?"

"Dude," Stamford said, rolling his eyes, "I know everything. *Everything.*"

"You're full of it," Connor said, taking another big swallow.

Stamford thumped the steering wheel in time to his words: "I. Am. So. Gonna. Score!"

"You're disgusting," Connor said, crushing his empty Lone Star can and throwing it at Stamford. It missed, bouncing off the driver's-side window.

Stamford didn't flinch.

"Kassie won't give you the time of day," Connor said, "much less a kiss—and most definitely not what you're after."

"You'll be crying," Stamford said. "You'll be crying hot tears of jealousy before Kassie leaves town."

Connor fumed.

———

In her letters, Kassie had told Connor he'd be the first to know when she was coming to town. But the letter he'd gotten from her two weeks ago had mentioned nothing about coming to Port Aransas. His stomach suddenly ached. Something was going wrong.

Stamford's fingers drummed the steering wheel, his gaze fixed on the Gulf.

Last summer, Connor had met Kassie before anyone else.

He'd decided to go surfing by himself, driving south from Avenue G. The waves were lame, so he randomly chose to stop about a mile down the beach. Nearby was a Chevrolet Suburban, with a tourist family sitting under a pole tent. Paying no attention to them, Connor had taken his board from the truck bed, walked down to the water, and was waxing it when a girl came over. He had looked up—and had been floored. She was absolutely stunning.

Connor had fought hard not to stare; his heart had suddenly started beating furiously. She introduced herself as Kassie, then asked a few questions about his board, the waves, and the Gulf. She was so beautiful that he'd barely managed to answer her.

Stamford started his truck, breaking through Connor's reverie. They backed away from the water, turned north, and started cruising back toward town.

The beach was deserted. No cars, no people, no buildings, just sand and grassy dunes on one side and sloshing beach break on the other—hundreds of miles of empty, sloshing beach break. Connor, still surreptitiously rubbing his arm, stared out the window at the waves. They'd driven ten miles south to where a large underground gas pipeline angled out from the beach, hoping that the waves there would jack up and get hollow as they rolled in over where the pipe was, but they never did. Certainly not like the Banzai Pipeline on the North Shore of O'ahu.

Depressing.

But Kassie Hernandez was something to be happy about. He had never met a girl as irreverent, fun, and brilliant as her.

Kassie was a complete NASA geek. Her dad had been one of the retrofire controllers on the Apollo missions. He was one of the guys who sent the trans-lunar burn instructions to the command module. Her dad had sprinted down to the basement at Mission Control when Apollo 13 blew its oxygen tank and had come back to the control room with a fat binder of procedures that outlined how to use the lunar landing module as a lifeboat.

And then there was the math savant thing. At a small party the summer before, everyone had been wasted—everyone but her. Two guys had been trying to calculate how much of a raise they should demand from the surf shop, but they were struggling because they didn't have a calculator.

"You don't need a calculator," Kassie told them. "I can multiply and divide anything in my head."

"Anything?" Stamford had asked, smirking. "I call bullshit. I don't believe it for a second."

"It's no bull," Kassie answered, her eyes lighting up.

"All right. What's three thousand six-hundred twenty-seven divided by one hundred and ninety-three?"

Kassie went quiet.

Stamford looked around at everyone.

"See?" he'd said. "She claims she's so smart, but it's bullshit."

"Eighteen point eight, rounded up," Kassie replied.

Everyone stared, then the room exploded in laughter.

"No way!" people shouted.

"Work it out," she said.

So the two guys divided it out on paper, then looked astonished.

"Holy shit!" one of them exclaimed. "She's right!"

That was a year ago. Connor had met her only a few days before her family went back to Midland. They sent letters back and forth, and Connor didn't like writing letters—but for her, well … and now she was coming to the beach once more, having graduated from high school as valedictorian of her class.

After fifteen minutes of driving, Stamford and Connor finally reached the Beach Lodge, a burger joint by day and a bar and hotel by night. Harley-Davidsons were parked outside, along with a few rust-bucket cars. Stains from old nails streaked down the weathered siding, while a tattered and faded horizontal banner fluttered stiffly in the breeze. Inside, a few ragged-looking folks sipped beer and smoked cigarettes, waiting their turn.

"Christ almighty," Stamford muttered.

When they finally reached Avenue G, Stamford fishtailed off the beach onto the asphalt.

"You know what?" he asked, grinning.

"What?"

Stamford paused for effect.

"I'm going to nail Kassie Hernandez."

"Oh, man," Connor said. "If she knew how much of a jackass slut you are, she'd run away as fast as she could."

Stamford was hated. He was hated not just because he could be an intolerable jerk, but because he could turn on a dime and be intolerably charming. He repeatedly scored with the best-looking tourist girls who came to the beach every summer. He could magically transform his personality on demand from a rube bastard to a suave sophisticate. He managed to play all kinds of bizarre intrigue with women. He would maneuver two girls against each other and get both. He'd played sister against sister, broken up girlfriends and boyfriends, and even pitted grown women against their belief in God. One spring break he managed to get all four girls staying in a single condo unit—one each day, for four days straight. The week after that, he had sex with a tourist girl one night and her mom the next morning—in the same hotel room.

"How immoral can one guy be?" Connor blurted out.

Stamford glanced at him, then pulled his Chevy Luv into the main driveway of Gulf Beach Cottages.

Angry from thinking about Stamford's adventures, Connor got out and grabbed his surfboard from the truck bed. On impulse, he walked up to Stamford's window and staked his claim: "Not this year, dude. This year Kassie will be mine. *All mine.* You'll be calling me 'Doctor Love' before she goes back to Midland."

Stamford looked at Connor for a moment, mouth agape in mock surprise, then hacked loudly and spat at Connor's feet.

"You're on," he said.

Then he cranked up AC/DC's "Whole Lotta Rosie," pumped his fist in the air, and drove away.

TWO

KASSIE HERNANDEZ LOOKED at her hair in the mirror, feeling disappointed. She frowned, regretting her decision to have her hair lightened. The stylist had made fake-looking streaks, with no subtlety whatsoever. But the feathering still looked good.

"Kassie," her mom called out, "what are you going to do about those scholarships?"

"Just a minute, Mom."

She decided to wear a T-shirt from Geri's Surfboard Shop. She tied it into a knot in front so it showed off her small silver belly stud. Everyone else stuck with earrings, but Kassie had seen some pictures in a cheap sci-fi magazine of Lieutenant Uhura in the *Star Trek* episode "Mirror, Mirror" sporting a belly button stud. Telling no one of her plans, Kassie found one for herself and got a piercing and her mom had just about died when she saw it.

Kassie turned and looked at herself. The white denim shorts contrasted sharply with her dark-brown skin. She imagined how she'd look with a mohawk, like her friend

Mark had gotten after becoming obsessed with the Sex Pistols.

Maybe guys would leave me the hell alone for once, she thought.

That made her laugh out loud.

She went into the living room. Her mom was sitting at the bar, sipping an old fashioned.

"San Diego," Kassie said.

Her mom frowned with exasperation.

"Honey, that's so far away from home. What about Tech?"

Her dad, sitting on the couch reading the *South Jetty*, lowered it and interjected: "Tech? No way. What about MIT?"

Kassie had made up her mind as soon as the UC San Diego offer had come in. That was the only school of the bunch that had her ideal combo: A great aeronautics program *and* close to the best waves on mainland America.

"Y'all both know San Diego's scholarship was the best. MIT didn't even come close."

Her dad smiled, but her mom's frown deepened.

"You just want to go *surfing*," Kassie's mom said, almost spitting the last word out of her mouth.

Kassie and her dad laughed.

"I'm going to a party for a while," Kassie said.

"You never stop, do you?" her mom replied.

"It's just a party, Mom. I won't be out late."

Her dad spoke firmly: "Eleven thirty. Not a minute later."

Kassie grinned. She knew he wasn't serious. Well, not too serious.

"I won't be long," she said, snatching her dad's car keys

from the kitchen counter. "I'll be home before this curfew thing, anyway."

She went out the door and skipped down the steps. The top of her dad's red '66 Corvair convertible was down. She got in and started it up, then pulled out of the Sea Isle parking lot. The wind blew her hair all to hell, but she didn't care.

Sandi from the surf shop had told her the party was at the Pod House. It was a weird home with polygon-shaped rooms, each elevated to an independent height by a central pylon.

Kassie knew Connor would be showing up. Sandi had connived with her to make sure Connor knew about the party, but *didn't* know Kassie would be there.

It had taken a huge amount of willpower for Kassie to hide from him that she was coming to Port Aransas—but, just like her dad, she loved practical jokes, and she wanted to surprise Connor. There were a lot of cute and fun surfer guys on the island, but he was the only guy she was really interested in—way too interested in. She needed to be careful. San Diego was calling, as was an aerospace engineering degree, which in her mind could lead to a job at NASA someday. It was all in the plan. Except for Connor. He could be *the* wrench in the works.

Kassie had kept Connor's letters in a desk drawer. She read them once, twice—and sometimes more than that. He'd even sent some photos, mostly of him with his surfboard or skateboard. All her friends thought he was cute. When they'd hung out last year, there had been none of those awkward silences, or any creepy male gaze, or the awful, unwanted touching. Instead, his eyes—*oh, my God, his eyes,* she thought—expressed actual interest in what she was talking about. He was a cool guy, excited about the ocean, surfing, skateboarding—and spaceships.

She especially liked one particular thing he'd written about: his love of bottlenose dolphins. He loved watching them jump and play in the water, and added it was cool when they swam up close to him while he was surfing. But the absolute best, he wrote, was watching them surf the same waves he was. Kassie remembered how scary it had been the first time a dolphin had come up close to her when she was surfing. She'd freaked out, thinking for a split-second that the big splash made by the huge animal had been a shark.

Kassie smiled at the memory.

Connor was just the opposite of the guys who catcalled when they saw her, the kind that made lewd gestures with their hands, the kind that always bellied right up to her—and then had jack all to say.

"Morons," Kassie muttered, shifting the Corvair into third and jabbing the gas pedal firmly.

Connor sat in his blue Toyota pickup truck drinking Lone Star, empty cans accumulating on the passenger floorboard. A few yards away, people went in and out of the party.

The house was built in the sixties and was the only upscale place on the island. Each pod had its own theme: Cave Room, Velvet Room, Starlight Room, Moon Room—and then the mirrored, red-velvet Love Room. Narrow hallways and spiral staircases connected the pods, and Hugh Hefner had partied there with Playboy Bunnies. The older islanders said the women had swum *nude* in the pools. There had been drinking, drugs—*orgies*.

Shadows moved in the windows; Connor felt gnawing panic. He had challenged Stamford, and Stamford would say anything at any time. Connor imagined it like this: He was with Kassie and Stamford, drinking, drinking—and at the critical moment Stamford would say: "Kassie, ol' Connor here was bragging that he's going to *bang* you this summer. He's calling himself *Doctor Love*. How 'bout that shit?"

But with each drink of beer, Connor's fears faded. His inner strength was growing. He could tell that, after this can of Lone Star, he'd have a full charge of confidence. When he went into the Pod House and saw Kassie, he'd know just what to do, just what to say—and just how to say it.

Some people walked past his car.

Connor sipped his last Lone Star, waited for the group of people to get up to the house and go through the gated fence. He felt ready.

You're on, Stamford, he thought, tossing the empty can on the floorboard.

Connor got out of his truck, walking fast.

Stamford would go down, he thought. He would stomp all over Stamford's ground and leave the party with Kassie. He would lead her away and shut the door in Stamford's face.

He was buzzed. He had to strike now.

Connor pushed open the gate and gazed upon the pool area, surveyed the bright uproar. Suddenly there was a shriek and a heavy splash, then laughter, and he saw a dark head pop up out of the lighted pool.

"You bastards!" the kid shouted.

There was more laughter and screeching as the victim tried to splash the perpetrators with water.

Connor skirted the commotion and entered the Pod House through the back door. The kitchen was filled with partiers.

"Sober up, asshole!" someone shouted.

Laughter followed from the young and the eager, those looking to get drunk or high, or to get laid—men, women, teenage girls, boys. It smelled of unclean underarm, patchouli, coconut tanning oil, and reefer.

Connor saw no sign of Kassie. Maybe she wasn't here yet. Maybe Stamford was wrong about when she was coming; maybe she wasn't coming at all. She would have told him, after all. Stamford probably was screwing with him, because that's how he operated. There was no kind of trick he wouldn't pull to get a cruel laugh. Connor edged past randoms and older people he barely knew. He tossed out head-nods, hey-dudes, and party-hardy greetings.

A voice bellowed over by the front door: "Kassayyy!!! Woooohooooo!!!!!"

Connor's heart started beating hard.

Damn, he thought—*she's here.*

He shrank down, edging away from the mobbing of Kassie, and darted up a curving, shag-carpet-covered stairway to the first floor. He kept going until he was half a level farther up. He headed through a corridor toward a quiet-looking room, where a few people stood just inside. Some had drinks in hand, but he couldn't tell who they were—shadows in the dark.

Standing at the door, he thought: *What the hell is wrong with me?*

He stepped boldly into the room—and the floor gave way.

He lurched forward and fell, crashing between two girls. He rolled over and looked up at them, bewildered, as something wet splashed onto his shirt.

"Asshole!" one of the girls yelled. "You made me spill my drink!"

She glared at him.

"What the hell?" he asked.

"It's the Moon Room, dipshit. The floor is soft, like the moon."

"Oh."

Connor crabbed backward away from them, then turned over and got up. His feet stabbed the soft floor, which only firmed up at the edge of the room. That's where he stood, trying to take stock of the situation. But he was nervous, shaking, crossing and uncrossing his arms. The girl who'd cursed him was casting the stink eye his way. She was hot, but she didn't like him—not at all. Connor gazed out the window as he tried to recover.

Kassie was downstairs, and he had to do something. Anything. He wished he had another Lone Star—and he had to talk to Kassie. Here she was, in Port Aransas. He'd sent her half a dozen letters, and she'd written even more in return, but she hadn't told him she was coming. That couldn't be good. He saw his dark reflection in the glass, then noticed a streetlight outside, all the while wishing he'd never said anything to Stamford.

You're a fucking moron, he said to himself.

"Connor!"

He turned to see Kassie standing in the doorway. Without waiting another moment, she stepped into the Moon Room—and pitched forward, out of control.

The contents of her drink shot straight through the air and hit the girl who'd cursed Connor right in the face. It splashed outward in all directions, sloshing over her chest and blotching her shirt. Kassie landed face-down at her feet.

"*Damn* it!" the girl yelled. She threw her cup to the side, snapped her blouse taught to see the stain. Fury distorted her face.

"Another *asshole!*" she shrieked.

Then she stormed out, followed by her friend, who pumped the finger up and down at Connor and Kassie while going out the door.

Connor stumbled over to Kassie and fell to his knees. She rolled over still holding her plastic cup, looking utterly disheveled, hair all over the place, mouth open, looking confused.

And stunning.

"Conner," she said, "did my drink just hit that girl in the face?"

"Yes."

For a moment, they were silent. Then they burst out laughing.

Connor took her in: Kassie wore short shorts, a Geri's Surfboard Shop T-shirt, and had a small silver stud in her belly button. His gaze lingered there. One of her flip-flops had been left behind at the door when she'd launched into the Moon Room. He felt a deep pressure flood through him; uncontrollably, his eyes traced over her, head to feet, then back again. Slow, deliberate—so she *knew*.

"Damn," he said, softly, and looked back into her eyes.

Her face turned serious.

"Like what you see?"

Connor's mouth parted slightly.

Impulsively, she put one arm around his head, gently pulled it down toward hers, and kissed him.

It was just like Kassie had imagined kissing him so many times alone in her room, when no one knew. Except now it was real. This kiss, this house, this moment. She tasted his salty clean mouth, and he tasted hers.

"Kassayyy!" shouted Stamford from the door.

They pulled apart.

"I told you to stay away from that man," Stamford said, walking over to them. "He's a bad, bad boy. Seriously, he's got designs on your body."

The spell broken, Kassie and Connor still looked at one another, surprised at what they'd just done.

Connor sensed Stamford's shadow looming, but he couldn't look away from Kassie. Then Stamford reached down and shoved him aside, so that he fell away from Kassie and sank into the Moon Room floor. Immobilized by the shock of the moment, he watched Stamford lead Kassie away. She looked back, smiling, but eyes uncertain, even confused—like she didn't understand what had happened, either. Stamford grabbed her derelict flip-flop on the way out as they disappeared down the hall.

THREE

THE MUSIC IS GOOD, *and the music is loud,* Connor thought.

He stood on the stairs in a daze looking down on the crowded kitchen. The record player blasted one hit song after the next. People stood in small groups, talking and drinking. He saw no sign of Kassie. In a stupor, he came down and joined his friends Robinson and Franklin.

Robinson swigged some beer, wiped his mouth with his hand. He smiled broadly. He was all freckles and dimples with a shock of wavy brown hair. Robinson had developed verbal ticks in grade school. Back then Stamford had asked: "Why do you talk like Bugs Bunny, man?" Robinson answered, "Eh—fuck you, Stamford."

Franklin was sometimes mistaken by girls for Joseph Cali, who played 'Joey' in Saturday Night Fever. Franklin had square shoulders and surfed so much that his upper body was chiseled like a Greek god, but his legs were so skinny that Connor sometimes had to bite his lip to keep from laughing when Franklin emerged from the water carrying his surfboard.

"There's a fuckton of hot chicks here tonight," Franklin said

"Shit, did you see those two who came with Maxim?" Robinson said. "Damn!"

"So why aren't you guys talking to any of these fucktons of hot chicks?" Connor asked.

Robinson flipped him off.

"Eh, fuck you, Connor. I oughta kick your ass."

Franklin spoke up: "Yeah, those chicks with Maxim were pretty hot, but not as hot as Kassie."

He nudged Connor's shoulder and pointed. Connor turned to look.

Kassie and Stamford were just coming out of a room. Her shirt was oddly twisted, like she had rushed to put it on, and she seemed disoriented or stoned. Stamford had a big smile on his face.

"Looks like Stamford just got laid," Franklin said.

"Maybe a blowjob," said Robinson.

"Bullshit," Connor replied.

"What's it to you, Connor? Robinson said. "You're not gonna get anywhere with Kassie. Besides, I *love* her."

"Everyone loves Kassie," said Connor. "There's no distinction in that."

The music had been shifting between extremes: Dire Straits, then AC/DC; Fleetwood Mac, then Foghat; ABBA, then Lynyrd Skynyrd. Now it was Joni Mitchell's turn. Connor saw that Stamford was all over Kassie. He was in overdrive, working it from every angle, talking, shouting, directing, touching, putting his arm around her. Kassie smiled distantly and nodded at his efforts, all the while maneuvering herself out from under his arm several times. Finally, she had enough. She looked at him with a frown, said something forceful—and Stamford, with a look of chagrin, stopped putting his arm around her.

Whatever Stamford had going on, it wasn't stopping other dudes from coming up to Kassie, even guys who had girls with them. Soon she was completely surrounded by gawkers and flirters, including Maxim, the surf shop manager, and Sandi, one of the foxes Maxim had brought with him. Sandi was right up next to Kassie, even holding her hand. They were laughing, but Kassie seemed to be looking around for somebody.

"Hey, Connor," Franklin said, "careful, or your eyes will burn holes right through Kassie's pants."

His friends laughed at him.

"Eh, what are you even thinking, Connor?" Robinson asked. "You've got zilch chance with Kassie. I mean, look—even Maxim is moving in."

Maxim was a resplendent Sammy Hagar look-alike. He wore a white linen shirt, unbuttoned, revealing his chiseled abs and pecs; he was a total hot body. Maxim smiled and talked to Kassie and Sandi with ease, telling them stuff that was making them laugh. Connor felt his confidence waning.

What's going on here? he thought. *Was that kiss she gave me for real, or was she teasing me because she was drunk or something? Am I just wishing things were true that aren't?*

After Joni Mitchell, somebody put on "I Saw Her Standing There" by the Beatles.

"Is this some kind of freaking joke?" Stamford shouted. "I mean, come on. This is the seventies, man."

"I love this song!" Kassie said. And with that, apparently everyone else did too—everyone except Stamford.

Maxim took Kassie by the hand and waved his arms at people to clear a small space. He started dancing to the song, and Kassie was all into it. Wildly, their bodies matched twist for twist, move for move. Behind them, Stamford's angry glare burned. On the other side of the room, Connor's pathetic disappointment showed plainly on his face.

And yet, while Kassie danced with Maxim, she kept looking over at him.

Robinson nudged Connor's arm.

"Eh, see that?" he said. "Kassie's looking at me!"

Franklin shot back: "Not at you, moron. She's actually looking at me!"

They argued, but Connor no longer heard. He was transfixed by Kassie: every twirl, every shuffle, every shake, every move she made....

When the song was over people hooted and Kassie disentangled herself from Maxim, sweaty and smiling. It was a smile that shot a pang of dread through Connor's heart. Maxim and Kassie had looked perfect dancing together, but when the song was over Maxim went to Sandi and kissed her.

Kassie turned to Connor and his friends, started laughing at them.

"What *are* y'all staring at?" she said, planting her hands on her hips.

"Eh," said Robinson.

"These guys were pretty thrilled by Maxim," Connor said. "But the only one I saw was you."

Kassie pointed at her sternum and tilted her head: "Me?"

Connor walked straight to her. It was totally out of character, but something about her attention on him made his uncertainty and doubt vanish. It was like another person inside him had taken control of what he was saying and doing.

"When you kissed me, I didn't ever want it to end," he said.

Eyes fixed on his, she said nothing.

Then they heard someone yell: "Tequila shots!"

Connor reached for Kassie's hand.

"Come on," he said.

She followed. At the bar there were a bunch of tequila shots on a tray. Connor took two and thrust one into her hand.

"To the best summer ever," he said, eyes glinting. They tapped their thin plastic shot glasses together, downed the tequila. Connor immediately grabbed two more. He saw Stamford across the room talking with one of Sandi's hot friends.

"Come on," Connor said to Kassie, leading her up the stairs.

Kassie had thought of Connor so many times over the last year, had written so many letters—more than he'd written to her. The letters had all been geeky stuff about NASA, science, and engineering. She'd revealed to him that she was taking flying lessons. None of it had been even remotely romantic, just stuff she might talk about with her brother—if her brother had half the brain in his head that Connor had in his.

Connor got Kassie in ways most guys didn't. He listened to her. He didn't constantly angle to make out with her or touch her in a "friendly" way while talking—none of that. They just talked about all the cool shit they loved.

When he unexpectedly let his eyes slowly roam over her body in the Moon Room, a sudden thrill pulsed through her. She loved being desired by *him*.

"Where are we going?" she asked.

"You'll see."

She liked it when he asserted himself and took her by the hand. *This was not the Connor from the letters,* she thought.

Maybe he was thinking about her at night, like she was thinking of him.

Connor stopped at the entrance to the Starlight Room and gave her one of the plastic shot glasses. The burn from the first one still lingered in her throat, and with the tequila on top of the drinks she'd had earlier, she was feeling a little buzzed.

"What do we toast to now?" she asked.

"Surfing. Let's drink to me teaching you how to surf."

Kassie struggled to keep a straight face.

"To the waves," she said. "And to you teaching me how to surf."

Connor saw her eyes glittering. He could tell she wanted to laugh.

"What is it?" he asked.

"Let's do it," she said, and held her arm out. "Put your arm through mine, then drink."

Connor entwined his arm through hers, and they drank. It was harsh. It burned. But they were face to face and very close and she could smell the tequila in the cups and on his breath. And surf wax, and coconut tanning oil. She looked at his puka shell necklace, then up to his face.

He smiled at her.

"Most the time, the waves are no good here," he said. "But maybe we'll get a storm in a few days. Even if it sucks, I want to see you tomorrow. Even if we don't go surfing."

Kassie downed her shot, wiped her mouth with a brown forearm, held up her empty shot cup. Connor took it, made a funny face at the two empty containers in his hand, tossed them both over his shoulder.

"Should we get more?" he asked.

Kassie pulled a crumpled piece of paper from her pocket. She gave it to Connor.

"That's my number here in Port A," she said. "You're going to call me, right?"

Connor stuffed the paper in his back pocket without looking at it. Downstairs, the stereo started playing again: "Love Hurts" by Nazareth.

For God's sake, not that one, Connor thought.

Kassie grinned.

"Perfect," she said. "Let's dance."

Connor put his arms around Kassie. She felt warm, firm, and she tucked into him perfectly; one of his hands gently pressed her head to his shoulder, the other moved around her waist. Connor's normal absurdly shy personality disappeared. He usually felt nervous even looking at a girl as hot as Kassie. She should be on TV—or in a movie.

Feeling him pressing against her, his heat, made Kassie's breath catch in her throat. It was like an ache, and it did not subside. It was like when she wanted to cry, but she didn't want to cry, this feeling was different. It was pure, fiery thrill. She turned her head up to look at him. In the dimly lit room she could tell he was looking past her, but he must have felt her looking up at him, because he looked down and met her gaze.

Connor felt the curves of her body pressing up against him. They fit together perfectly. Unable to help himself, he gently kissed her upturned forehead. It was the natural thing. In response, it seemed like Kassie held him tighter and pressed her hips into him even more. Hoping she'd lift up and kiss him, Connor pulled back a little to look at her. But instead of kissing him, she asked a question.

"The letters," she said. "When you wrote them to me, did you feel what I know you're feeling right now? Did you think of me like this when you wrote those letters?"

"Yes," Connor said. "I thought about you every day. I

wanted to write you every day. I didn't want to freak you out, though, so when I did write I didn't say some of the things that I was thinking about."

"But you weren't lying? You weren't just pretending to be interested in all the things I wrote about: the space program, working at NASA someday, flying, all that?"

"Everything I wrote was the truth," he replied. "I just kept some things to myself."

There was a brief pause in their whispered talk, the song's guitar solo wailing mournfully. They clutched each other tenderly, a tension building inside both of them like the beginnings of something that might change the paths they were on.

"I've thought about you, Connor," Kassie said. "I've thought about you a lot."

She pressed her hips against his, rotated them very slightly to match the music so it wasn't too obvious, but that he would know what she was feeling. All the thoughts she'd ever had about being friends with Connor—all those interests of his that seemed to match interests of hers—dissolved. They didn't mean a damn thing to her in that moment. She felt him lightly kiss her forehead again, so gentle. She couldn't help herself. She turned her face upward, stretched up, closed her eyes. Their lips met. His hand grasped her long hair at the nape of her neck, pulled just a touch, and she felt a chill she'd only ever imagined. In this perfect moment, it felt like all she had ever wanted was him, and him—*and him.*

Suddenly there was a sound of a record player needle scratching heavily across black vinyl. Some drunk had tried to grab the record arm but missed the mark. The music had stopped. Shouts and curses from downstairs spoiled the moment.

"Damn it, dude!" they heard a man yell. "I'm going to beat your ass into the sand for that!"

"Fuck off, asshole!" they heard Stamford shout. "Nazareth is bullshit!"

"What's going on?" Kassie said. "Is that Kevin?"

"Yup," sighed Connor. "That's Stamford."

The commotion downstairs turned to raucous pandemonium. Furniture was crashing over, followed by loud thuds and bumps. A woman shrieked. There was a brief pause, then it sounded like a bottle shattered. A man yelled in pain.

Kassie let go of Connor abruptly and turned, hurried toward the door.

"Wait!" Connor yelled.

But she was gone.

"Fucking Stamford," he muttered, then followed Kassie out the door.

Downstairs, Connor saw Stamford and a longboard guy from Corpus who sometimes surfed at Horace Caldwell Pier slugging each other. A tight ring of people surrounded them, shouting faces. Kassie was trying to get through the crowd.

"Kevin!" she shouted. "Kevin!"

Stamford grabbed the guy's shoulder-length hair and started swinging him around in circles, trying to throw him off balance. Head down, the guy was swinging his fists wildly, trying to hit Stamford, but his arms weren't long enough. At last the Corpus dude spun free, stepped to his right and threw a left, hitting Stamford square in the chest. Stamford tumbled backward into a clump of girls. They scattered, yelling, as a fist swung out of nowhere and hit the guy from Corpus in the eye.

Maxim!

Connor stood, open-mouthed. It was like a cliché movie scene: Multiple dudes started swinging, and the next thing Connor knew Stamford threw a barstool at the dude from Corpus. It hit him, but then bounced and hit two other guys. Stamford stood tall, laughing at them, then got grabbed from behind, and they all went down to the floor. A din of shouting and cursing erupted. A girl screamed, another bottle shattered.

The revelers started running. Connor saw Kassie for a moment in the melee, then got bowled over by Maxim dragging his two girlfriends, one in each hand, toward the door.

"The cops, Connor!" he shouted over his shoulder. "The cops are gonna bust everybody they can catch!"

"Cops!" other people shouted. "It's the cops!"

A stampede began. Connor was shoved by the crowd toward the door, wondering what was happening to Kassie and if his other friends were still in the middle of the fight or if there even was a fight anymore.

Outside, he heard distant sirens, one coming from the harbor area and another coming from the direction of the beach.

There was no time. He stood for a moment by the gate near the pool. People ran past, knocking into him as he tried to find Kassie, but she was nowhere to be seen. The sirens blared louder.

Connor ran.

He hoofed it down the street with everyone else, scores of feet pounding asphalt, running past lines of parked cars. Some were firing up, headlights turning on. People were piling into other cars, screaming, bitching, laughing.

Connor jumped in his Toyota and started it, rolled down one window to listen for the cops, then gunned it down the first side street he came to. It was empty. He zigzagged down a few streets, considered turning his lights off. As soon as he turned onto the cutoff road a cop car zoomed past him in the opposite direction toward the Pod House. If his lights had been off, he'd have gotten busted. Connor kept going, heart racing, but forced himself to cruise under the speed limit, eyes glancing between the road and the review mirror.

Moments later, he pulled into the drive at Gulf Beach Cottages and parked in front of the first unit. Cars sat in front of all the other cottages, but this first one was empty. He turned off the ignition and the lights.

He grinned, still feeling the sharp high of fright, a little out of breath, his heart beating fast.

He had escaped.

It was a cool night. His window was down. He could hear the Gulf's low roar. The air was wet with saltwater mist. He watched the moisture of the sea blurring the front windshield.

Connor leaned back and closed his eyes. Desire ruled his brain; visions of Kassie filled it. One hand rested on his forehead, the other cupped his nuts.

FOUR

TROPICAL DEPRESSIONS and hurricanes did things for Port Aransas surf that hundreds of miles of wind fetch in the Pacific did for the surf on the North Shore of O'ahu.

When the waves got big and mean, it scared everybody, but no one admitted it; instead, they hooted and hollered and stamped around swirling towels and talking about how stoked they were. The serious guys got out their Gulf navigation charts and plotted the positions of each storm, noting its course and direction, and how fast it was moving. Close attention was paid to wind speed and temperature. They speculated about trips to South Padre or Galveston, or up toward Louisiana—wherever they thought the waves would be biggest.

The long, dark lines would march toward shore. The surfers would wait for them, the bigger the waves, the farther out they'd have to paddle. Past the third sandbar, all they could see of the beach was the tips of the dunes. When they were a couple hundred yards past the end of the pier, in water twenty feet deep, Connor and his friends felt an emptiness in the pit of their stomachs. No one spoke of it, but everyone knew that sometimes an angler would reel in a fifteen-foot hammerhead at the pier.

With hurricanes, the waves could build into green walls twelve to fifteen feet high, and they felt the power of them in their bones. The thrashing whitewater avalanches terrified them. Going over the falls would be the end. But those were the days that mattered. Perfect, uncrowded waves for all—miles and miles of perfect waves. Someday it would come. And they would be ripping when it did.

Connor called Kassie's number the next day around 10 a.m., but nobody answered. He called again at 2 p.m. Still no answer. He stared out the window of his room at the palm fronds shaking in the heavy onshore winds, bit his lip, and called again.

"Hello?"

It was Kassie.

"Hey," he said. "It's me."

"Connor?"

"Yeah."

"Oh, God, I'm glad you called. Yesterday was crazy. My dad grounded me! Can you believe that?"

"Grounded?"

"Yeah, I came back two hours past curfew."

"Curfew?"

"I don't know. I never had curfew before. I forgot all about it. Right when I was leaving for the party, my dad said be home at 11:30 and ... well, whatever, never mind.

Anyway, they don't even want me talking on the phone. They went out for a minute. Did you try to call before?"

"Yeah, I ..."

"Connor, I think they're coming back up the stairs now. I gotta go. Call me later?"

But Kassie hung up before Connor could answer.

Pelican's Wharf was one of the best restaurants in town. It could go from a chill, laid-back restaurant with just a few tables of guests to a full-on dinner rush in a matter of minutes. When the Deep Sea Roundup or other big fishing tournament weekends rolled around, it was near mayhem, with the line for a table snaking out the door and into the parking lot. Cocktail waitresses would walk along the line, taking orders and bringing drinks outside to fisherman who were bragging, laughing, yelling.

For attire, everyone except the cocktail waitresses and hostesses had to wear flowered Hawaiian print shirts. No flowered shirt, no work.

Al "The Bear" Higgens, Connor's boss, was the manager and cook. He was large, hairy, and always looked tired—but Al had *moves*. At peak rush, he became a tornadic ballet of food production. In a matter of minutes, he could cover the grill with steaks, shrimp, beef kebabs, and marinated chicken breasts. He also managed two hundred spuds in the oven, scores of artichokes and gallons of Alaskan king crab in the steamers. The restaurant sold fresh-caught red snapper and a French-inspired dish called seafood coquille. Australian lobster tails were roasted in the broiling ovens. Al slammed doors, spun about, sweated, poured ladles of butter. He scraped the grill with a big wire brush between layering it with food, covering his hand and arm with a dirty towel. The flames would shoot to the ceiling and spread out in a mushroom cloud with each stroke across the grill.

When food was ready for a table, Al would reach up, yank the clapper of a head-sized bell that hung on the side of the kitchen. *BING!* He would stare with his black eyes out into the restaurant, irritated that a waiter wasn't already scooping the plates up to take to the table. Steak, baked potatoes, wild rice pilaf—if he saw the food getting cold he got angry. He busted his ass to get food to the customers quickly, his concentration unrelenting and unmatched, his flowered shirt stained with sweat.

Al told the wait staff: "The order is ready when the bell rings—and when the bell rings, the order is *ready*. Got that?"

Any waiter who didn't got fired.

Connor became the most efficient waiter. He snatched his tables' plates from the serving bar and stacked them up his arm, carried them to the table, doled them out. Often the bell would ring again—"Order up!"—before he even had the last table's plates delivered.

Connor saw Kassie and Stamford on his way back to the kitchen after getting an order from a party of twelve.

Kassie was wearing a short, white skirt, a blouse showing cleavage, and white sandals with matching straps that wound around her calves.

She looks like a Greek goddess, he thought.

When she saw Connor, she brightened immediately, then waved at him and smiled.

In contrast, Stamford—in a rumpled T-shirt, jeans, and slaps—glared at him.

"Hoped you wouldn't be here," he blurted.

Kassie shot Stamford an irritated look.

Connor forced a smile at them before rushing back to the

serving bar, where Al gave him the stink eye. Connor tried to focus on delivering the next order; he tried to not think about what he had just seen. But his heart had just been run through with a dagger of ice.

Luckily, he didn't have to walk past Stamford and Kassie to deliver the order. After getting the customers situated and happy, he retreated back past the bus station and into the walk-in cooler. There he grabbed a Lone Star and slammed some, not even wincing at the ice cream headache.

Fuck it, he thought. *Isn't she supposed to be grounded?*

She had lied to him. Why didn't she just tell him the truth, that she had a date with Stamford? Connor took another slug of beer.

"Maybe she's not as simple and honest and true as she seems to be," he mused out loud.

The bell rang. He heard Al's muffled voice: "Order up!"

Connor admitted to himself that he and Kassie hadn't hung out very much—hardly at all, in fact—and he didn't even really know who she was. And just look at her: How could he have even the slightest chance with a girl as hot as she was? Even the letters she'd written, which seemed to show they had a lot in common, now seemed misleading. It didn't make sense. What about their dancing, their kissing? What the hell was going on?

The dinner bell clapped again, hard, and this time Al said nothing—a bad sign.

"Shit," muttered Connor, downing the last of the beer.

He could always hope they wouldn't be seated in his section.

But sure enough, within twenty minutes they appeared at the only two-top Connor had.

He had no choice, so he grabbed a couple of menus and headed over, forcing a smile.

"You don't seriously believe all that crap?" Stamford asked Kassie as Connor arrived.

Kassie laughed, but Connor recognized that she was scoffing at what Stamford had said.

"What are you talking about?" she retorted, her eyes wide, her brow in a frown.

"Armstrong and Aldrin didn't step out onto the moon. They stepped out onto a soundstage. Total Hollywood bullshit."

Kassie said nothing.

"Hey, guys," Connor said. "How's it going?"

Stamford gave him a harsh look.

"Do you want a broken nose?" he asked Connor.

Kassie's mouth dropped open.

"You did not just say that."

Connor, feeling emboldened, looked at her and explained: "That's bad Kevin's idea of a joke. How about you guys take a look at the menu—and since you're both over eighteen, I'll get the cocktail waitress to come over and get your drink orders."

Stamford took the menu and glared at it, while Kassie smiled guiltily at Connor.

"My dad let me off the hook," she said, trying to lock eyes with Connor, but he avoided her gaze. The bell rang hard.

"Order up!"

"Welp," Connor said. "I'll be back."

He walked off, knowing that Stamford, the most cheapskate dude of all time, was wincing as he looked at the menu. If there were any silver lining to him taking Kassie on a date—or even getting her back to his shambles of an apartment to have sex with her—it was that he would have to pay more money than he wanted to get the job done.

Kassie was embarrassed. She knew Connor worked at Pelican's Wharf, but Kevin had cornered her unexpectedly at Geri's Surfboard Shop the day before. She'd gone there to get some beachwear, and to get the details about the party from Sandi.

He'd had come in, started gabbing with them, and when Sandi went to the business office briefly, Kassie had been taken off guard by his sudden and smooth offer to eat at Pelican's Wharf together—as friends. She was annoyed, she hesitated, the last thing she wanted right then was to be accosted by a guy wanting a date. But after a bit of back and forth with him, she realized it would be easier to get out of Geri's faster by equivocating. Like many of her friends, she had learned it was often easier to bail later over the phone than deal with pushy guys in person—and Kevin Stamford pushed hard.

"I have to see if my mom and dad have plans tonight," she'd told him.

But afterward part of her had rationalized that going to Pelican's with Kevin might reduce the threat of Connor O'Reilly derailing her hard-won plan for college. So when he called later in the afternoon, she'd ignored her gut feelings.

"I've always wanted to eat there," she said on the phone, feeling almost numb. "As long as we're going as just friends, like you said at Geri's. I mean, I have a boyfriend in Midland, you know."

"Absolutely. I'll pick you up at six thirty."

The boyfriend excuse was untrue, but handy. She had already started breaking up with Andrew, the boy she'd been casually dating for most of high school. For her, it had never been serious, though the whole school—and even Andrew—

seemed to believe she was destined to be an oilfield wife after high school, valedictorian or not.

Now here she was, sitting at dinner with Kevin Stamford. He was good-looking, for sure, but she had no feelings for him—none. So, zero risk. Connor, on the other hand was high risk; her feelings for him were way too strong. A boyfriend in Port A *and* a full-ride scholarship at UC San Diego? It seemed impossible. But right now she was angry at the decisions she'd made that led her to sitting at this table with Kevin Stamford instead of waiting outside the restaurant later on for Connor to be off work. In that moment, she wanted to have Connor all by herself in a parked car on the beach. Then she could find out what was real.

"What's going on in that beautiful head?" Stamford asked. "You look like you're thinking about something you really like."

She looked up to meet Stamford's questioning gaze. The candle on the table flickered, and a puff of smoke wafted up. She could smell the burning wick.

"Nothing, really," Kassie said, stirring her piña colada before changing the subject.

"So you say Armstrong and Aldrin were on a sound stage?" she asked.

Stamford straightened up, frowned a little.

"Yeah. That's what I said."

"It looked real to me."

Kassie let her eyes linger on the steamed artichoke that Connor had placed on the table next to her. There was a ramekin of melted butter alongside a ramekin of mayonnaise.

"Where were all the stars?" Stamford asked.

"Where are the stars during the day on Earth?" she countered.

"At night you see stars in space because the sky is black,"

Stamford replied. "But there are no stars in those Apollo movies. The sky is black. No stars. So it's fake."

"Too much light," Kassie explained. "Just like on Earth during the day."

"But the sky is *black*, Kassie. There should be stars in it."

Kassie thought her eyebrows might lift completely off her face in astonishment.

"*Oh-kay*," she said.

She selected one of the artichoke leaves and plucked it gently from the stem, regarding it slowly as she turned it this way and that. Then she looked directly into Stamford's eyes.

"I am sure," she purred, "that it was every bit as real as this artichoke leaf."

She dipped the leaf in the mayo, dipped it in the butter, lasciviously placed it in her mouth and slowly withdrew it, making a face of ecstasy. She dropped the tooth-scraped leaf on her side plate, then let the butter dribble a little bit out of the side of her mouth. It ran down in a streak and lingered on her chin.

"*Mmmmm*," she said, letting her eyelids narrow. She wiped the butter off her lip and chin with a finger, then stuck her finger in her mouth and sucked it clean. She pulled it out, regarded it thoughtfully.

"Tastes good," she said. "Definitely real. Too bad we don't agree on what's real, Kevin."

Connor had spent the absolute minimum amount of time possible waiting on them. The more he thought about Kassie not telling him the truth, the more upset he got. But at the same time, he was jealous of Stamford and spied on their date when he thought they wouldn't notice.

I'm the one that should be eating dinner with her, he thought. *Not Stamford.*

As Connor watched, they'd gone from talking a lot—very animated—to eating their food in silence.

Stamford signaled Connor for the check while Kassie was still eating, but Connor kept busy with other things until it seemed like Kassie was done. She flashed a big smile at him when he took their plates. Connor quickly added up their bill and took the check to the table. Stamford grabbed it, looked at it, then set it on the table and pushed it toward Kassie.

She smirked, knowing without asking what he wanted. She glanced briefly at the bill, instantly tallying the amounts, even before Connor had turned and walked away. Before he was out of earshot, Connor heard Kassie tell Stamford: "My part's eighteen dollars and fifty-three cents, including a twenty percent tip for the waiter."

Connor busted a huge smile, stifling a laugh. He knew what was coming.

"Twenty percent? That's crazy. Let me see that bill."

Connor had never seen Stamford blowing it this bad. His usual incredible ability to charm women had somehow evaporated—and while Connor was busy serving other tables, he noticed Stamford hunched over the bill with a pen, doing the math, trying to verify Kassie's numbers.

The bell clanged again, signaling that Connor had more food to deliver. Before he got back from that chore, Kassie and Stamford had left, so he went to the table and collected the bill. He opened the folder to find cash for Stamford's part, with no tip at all. But Kassie had paid with a fifty-dollar bill— way more than a twenty percent tip.

But that's not what made Connor stop in his tracks. What made him freeze was the handwritten note on the back of the tab:

I'm sorry, Connor. I wish I had been eating dinner with you instead of your friend. Can I see you when you get off work? (We were NOT on a date!!!) I'll be at Boxcar Billy's. Don't forget your offer to give me surfing lessons. How about tomorrow? Aren't the waves supposed to be better at sunrise?
:)
xoxo — Kassie

FIVE

BOXCAR BILLY'S was where they went after the restaurants closed to knock back Lone Stars, Buds, and liquor to anesthetize for the coming day of fishing, manual labor, and then more partying. Boxcar Billy's was new, so lots of islanders were eager to hang out there. They were tired of the same old places, so even a legend like Shorty's was abandoned—at least temporarily—for Boxcar Billy's.

When Connor walked in, he saw a crowd of people hovering around the shuffleboard table—and there was Kassie, leaning over it. She pushed one of the metal pucks down the table with a flourish.

It went straight into the gutter.

"Aw," she said.

"I'll show you how it's done, darlin.'" Stamford pushed a puck down the table. It glided true and bumped another one of his pucks, moving both into a higher scoring zone.

Connor went to the bar to get a beer. While he waited for the bartender to get him a cold one, he felt a warm presence near him, smelled the same Yves Saint Laurent fragrance he'd noticed at Pelican's.

It was Kassie.

Connor turned to face her.

"Hey," she said, almost sadly.

Connor smiled.

"I'm sorry about tonight," she said. "It was a mistake."

"No, no," he said. "It's all right. I didn't know you were dating Stamford."

Kassie's eyes narrowed.

"Don't say that," she said.

Connor laughed.

"Sorry," he said. "I thought you were grounded."

Kassie didn't like what Connor said, but his feelings were hurt—and she had hurt them. Knowing that made her feel tense.

"Connor, he just wouldn't leave me alone until I said I'd let him take me to the best restaurant in town—as friends," she explained. "I did it just to get him off my back. I'm sorry about the grounding thing. I was grounded, but I weaseled out—and then I felt obliged to honor eating with Stamford at Pelican's. I wasn't able to let you know what was going on. I'm sorry."

Connor noticed that she had referred to Stamford by his last name, like everyone else did. She put her hand on his elbow, looked at him square in the eyes.

"Think you can forgive me?" she asked.

Kassie seemed sincere, and Connor wasn't ready to blow his chance with her, but just as he was about to say that he forgave her, he was interrupted by a shout from Stamford over by the shuffleboard table.

Startled, they both turned and looked.

Connor thought that maybe Stamford had been insulted

that Kassie wasn't at his side, and that he was going to make trouble. Instead they saw him celebrating a win, collecting money from his opponents.

"Two out of three," one of his opponents said.

"Only if I play you guys by myself," he replied.

During the negotiations, Connor looked back at Kassie, who smiled at him.

"Hey," said the bartender, irritated at Connor. "That'll be a buck fifty."

"Want a drink?" Connor asked Kassie.

"Yeah. Gimme a Lone Star," Kassie told the bartender. "I'm buying for both of us."

"Well, thanks, darlin'," said Connor. "I didn't know you liked Lone Star."

"I prefer tequila," she said, smiling. "And don't call me 'darlin'. I hate that."

Before Connor could think of an answer, the bartender put another Lone Star down on the bar. Kassie paid with a five-spot.

"Keep the change," she said.

"Well, thanks, darlin'," the bartender said as he turned away.

Kassie raised her bottle in mock salute to the bartender.

Connor laughed.

"Seems you have an unwanted nickname."

Kassie frowned.

"Clink bottles?" she asked. "Forget and move forward? Move to where we'd rather be right now?"

Connor's heart skipped a beat. He wondered if she meant he should move to San Diego with her.

They clinked their bottles together, then raised them up high and guzzled before lowering them at the same time, wiping their mouths with their hands. That made Kassie laugh.

"Synchronized beer drinking," she said. "Maybe we're something of a match?"

Connor had already swallowed his beer but now he swallowed a sudden ache in his throat that became a burn in his stomach—a burning desire for Kassie Hernandez.

"I say let's go surfing tomorrow," he said. "It's not supposed to be big surf. Perfect for beginners. What do you think?"

Kassie's face lit up.

"I've always wanted to try," she said. "I used to watch from the beach when we lived in Hawaii."

"Hey, you didn't tell me you lived in Hawaii in your letters. What's up with that?"

"My dad worked the Gemini flights as a remote CapCom and tracker out there. I'd go over to the North Shore and watch the surfers. I was just a kid, though."

"No autographs from Gerry Lopez or Rory Russell?"

"Gerry's a really nice guy," she said.

Connor stared.

"Don't tell me you know Gerry Lopez."

Kassie laughed.

"Well, not really, no," she said. "I mean, to him I was just a random gremmie. He didn't know my name or anything like that."

"Gremmie? What are you saying here? You're kidding me, right?"

Kassie laughed again.

"Did I use the word 'gremmie' wrong?" she asked. "I thought it was just Hawaiian for 'kid.' "

"Sort of," Connor replied, getting suspicious.

He was about to ask her more about Hawaii when they heard a huge yell come from the shuffleboard table.

"That's right, losers!" they heard Stamford shout. "Time to pay the piper, baby. Hand it over. I need that money to make up for a crappy dinner at Pelican's."

He smirked before looking over at Kassie and Connor.

"Well, Stamford's getting drunk," Connor said, "and that's not always a nice thing. Tell me: He didn't give you a ride to dinner, did he?"

"Unfortunately, yes," Kassie replied. "I would have taken my dad's car and met him there, but my mom and dad went over to Corpus to see a movie."

Connor watched Stamford collect his winnings before heading to the jukebox to put some quarters in, and ZZ Top's "La Grange" started playing. He turned and came to them, exaggerating some hip jutting and shuffling in time to the beat of the song.

"Well, how about the two love birds," he said, in a deep Billy Gibbons imitation—and then, in time to the music: *"A-hah-hah-hah!"*

Stamford was positively steamed on Jack and Coke.

"Dude, we're just talking," Connor said, frowning.

"I know," said Stamford. "I mean, it's not like you could get anywhere with Kassie anyway."

Nobody said anything to that while Billy Gibbons sang undeterred from the jukebox.

Then Connor said: "Get this, dude. Kassie knows Gerry Lopez."

Stamford looked sideways, furrowing his brow.

"Damn," he said. "I mean ... how do you know him? Did you live on the North Shore or somethin'?"

"Yeah, well, I just saw him on the beach sometimes," Kassie said. "Sometimes over at Kammie's."

Stamford's mouth was agape. Then his face relaxed, and he looked off in the distance.

"Man, I'd so dig knowing Gerry Lopez. That guy can surf. Best style ever."

"No way, man," Connor said. "Buttons all the way!"

Kassie listened silently as the two bickered about which North Shore surf star was better.

It's ridiculous to rate Gerry Lopez against Buttons Kaluhiokalani, she thought. She was irritated by Stamford's presence. She wanted to hang out with Connor alone. Growing frustrated as they argued, she took a big swig of beer and interrupted them.

"I'm sick of smelling the nasty smoke in here," she said. "I'm going outside."

She touched Connor on the elbow and smiled at him before setting her empty Lone Star on the bar. Then she walked out the door to join some people who were standing around in the parking lot.

Connor and Stamford watched her leave.

"I think I need to go outside," Connor said.

"Whatever," Stamford said. "I'm having second thoughts about scoring with her anyway."

"Oh?"

"Yeah. She's a damned know-it-all."

"Well," Connor said, "what I know is that Buttons and Larry Bertlemann are the future of surfing. Same with Rabbit and Shaun. Gerry's a legend, but these new guys are busting down the door."

"Shit," Stamford replied. "Kassie will claim she knows all those guys, too. It's just bullshit. She just wants to fuck with us."

"I dunno, man."

"As long as she says so, huh?" Stamford asked, wagging his head like a bobbleheaded dash ornament.

"I think I'll go outside, man," Connor said. "Too much smoke blowing. It's getting to me."

"Good company out there," Stamford said, nodding toward the door. "Good company if you like lying-ass bullshit cock teasers."

What Connor saw in the tiny parking lot almost made him stop in his tracks: Kassie was standing by Maxim, who had his arm around her shoulders, while Sandi was under his other arm. Kassie looked perfectly comfortable. She wasn't pulling away, didn't seem put off at all like she had been with Stamford clawing all over her at the Pod House.

Maybe Maxim managed to seduce her while they were dancing at the party, Connor thought. *Maybe now he's moving in for the score.*

Connor didn't know. The sight had sent a shock through him, like a bucket of ice water had been dumped over his head.

He remembered what Robinson had said at the party: *What was he even thinking? How could he believe all of the things she was telling him? Didn't they seem a little farfetched? Buzz Aldrin coming over to their house in Houston to study trans-lunar burns with her dad? Gerry Lopez?*

There were limits to his gullibility. And now another dude was nuzzling up all over her. For a moment, he felt like walking back to his truck and leaving.

Fuck that, said a voice inside Connor's head. *No way are you giving up.*

This was total opposition, pure competition. He wasn't

going to just walk away from his challengers. Not from Stamford, not from Maxim, not from anybody. So he went over and stood a few feet in front of Kassie, looking right at her, the shock still strong inside him.

As soon as Kassie noticed Connor, she untangled herself from Maxim, who didn't seem to care. He just kept talking to Sandi, his main squeeze, not visibly reacting to Kassie's departure.

"I was starting to think you hadn't gotten the hint in there," Kassie said, stepping up.

"What?"

"I don't like rude drunks, but I do like good-looking surfer guys."

"Maxim?"

Kassie laughed.

"I'm not looking at him, am I?" she said.

Kassie moved until she was almost pressing up against him. On tiptoe, she leaned into his ear to whisper: "I need you to please give me a ride home, Connor O'Reilly."

Maxim, who wasn't used to having women detach themselves from under his arm to go over to the likes of Connor O'Reilly to whisper in their ear, was impressed. He thought maybe Connor was coming into his own at last, and he liked it. Maxim smiled and nodded at him.

Kassie stood back down flat on her feet, but she remained very close to Connor. He could feel the pressure of her presence—and he liked it.

"I can't wait to go surfing with you tomorrow," Kassie said. She finished off her beer and set it down on the asphalt parking lot.

"It's gonna be fun," he said, and took another swig of Lone Star. "Let me finish this off and we'll go."

"I'd like that," she said. Then, to Connor's amazement, she put her hand in his free one and gently held it.

Maxim was now watching closely—a bit shocked maybe, but he really dug it. Kassie had left him, gone to Connor, and whispered in his ear. Now she was holding his hand. Maxim was surprised because she had been responding really well to his flirtation. But he could see that Kassie had something for Connor, and that pleased him. He liked that shy Connor suddenly had enough mojo to get a girl like Kassie interested in him. Besides, he figured, sharing was always possible.

"Well, what the fuck," Stamford bellowed, staggering out the door.

Everyone outside turned to look at loudmouthed Stamford.

"I mean, I brought this Lone Star out here for you, Kassie," he said, "but it looks like you've gotten a little distracted."

"I'm not distracted," she said. "I know exactly what I want and exactly what I'm doing."

"So you just blow off the guy who took you to dinner?"

"Are you kidding me?" she asked Stamford. "You didn't take me to dinner. You shoved the check across the table and told me to pay up. Then you made me pay the whole tip. That's no kind of date, Kevin Stamford."

Everybody except Stamford laughed.

"So this is the problem," he said, with a hint of threat. "You think you can just grab one guy after the next and use 'em because you're so hot. Well, it doesn't work that way 'round here."

Stamford meant to move toward them, but lurched drunkenly instead. Kassie backed up half a step, weary, but not cringing. She turned slightly sideways. Without thinking about what he was doing, Connor stepped between them.

"Come on, dude," Connor said. "Just cool it. I mean, it's not like you can seriously accuse anyone of being loose."

"Oh, that's how it is, now, Connor?" Stamford asked. "I oughta kick your ass right here in front of your new girlfriend."

In that moment, a passing cop car swerved suddenly, did a U-turn, then pulled into the parking lot. The car lurched as the cop hit the brakes. The headlights shone bright on them all, casting their shadows across the building. Everyone who had a beer quietly put their bottles down.

Everybody but Stamford.

The cop got out, clicked on his flashlight, pointed it at Stamford, who squinted, turned his head away. In each of his hands was an open bottle of beer.

"What's that you got there, son?" the cop asked.

Stamford raised his arms up just above his head.

"A two-fist salute, brother."

The cop was new. None of them had ever seen him before.

"Son, maybe you should have done like the rest of your friends here and put those beers down when I pulled up."

"Why's that, big man?"

The cop moved fast. He went straight to Stamford, grabbed one of his arms and yanked him backward. Both beers fell onto the parking lot, one breaking, the other spewing foam.

"Hey, pig," Stamford screeched. "What the fuck?"

"Dude, you're being a moron," Maxim said forcefully. "Just apologize, and I'll take you home."

"He's got a ride home," said the cop, who yanked Stamford toward the squad car.

Stamford tried to struggle.

"Don't be a complete dipshit," yelled the cop.

But, in that moment, Stamford became a shining light of idiocy. He struggled and tried to yank violently away from the cop. He failed, loudly yelling and crying.

"This is so unfair. You're hurting me!"

"Shut the hell up," the cop said. "If you had any brains, this wouldn't be happening to you."

The cop shoved Stamford into the back of the police car and slammed the door. Then, before getting in and carting Stamford off to the Port Aransas jail, he paused at the driver's-side door and pointed his flashlight at the group of them.

"Your buddy should've learned from y'all's fine example. Maybe tomorrow you can teach him how to not get arrested."

The cop got in, slammed his door, and backed out of the parking lot. He gunned the motor and drove west toward Alister Street, running through the stop sign at Station, and in a brief streetlight flash they saw Stamford's shadow pounding on the grate between the back seat and where the cop sat behind the wheel.

One by one, people picked up their beers and started drinking again.

"Well, that was fun," Maxim said.

SIX

"LET'S drive down the beach and look at the waves," Connor said as they backed out of Boxcar Billy's. "There's always a chance it'll be better than just two-foot slop in the morning."

"Sure," Kassie said.

Connor felt nervous. He didn't know what to think: Kassie at the party with him, at Pelican's with Stamford, with Maxim's arm over her shoulders at Boxcar Billy's, then holding his hand and driving away with him. He thought of all the letters they'd written. Sometimes it felt like he had known her all his life, and other times it felt like she was a complete stranger. Who was she? Who else had she been with? How many? It might have been absurd for a guy like Stamford to call her a slut, and it pissed Connor off—but, then again, Kassie could snag any dude she wanted.

"It was sweet of you to step between me and Stamford," Kassie said.

"I wasn't going to let him do anything to you."

"Like I said, it was sweet. I wouldn't have let him hurt me."

Connor glanced over at her. The statement had been absolutely matter of fact, as though there weren't the slightest chance in hell of Stamford being able to hurt her.

"He was an ass for implying you were loose with guys."

"Sometimes I feel loose," she said.

"What do you mean?" he asked.

"Look at me," she said.

He looked.

"What do you see?"

Connor saw absolute, pure sexual power.

"I mean you're a fox, Kassie. But I don't see you only like a —"

"Fox?" she completed his sentence as a question. "Well, that's pretty much all other people see. I'm a fox, they say. I'm hot. After a while, you get sick of hearing that stuff."

Connor laughed with shock.

"I don't know, Kassie. I think I could kinda get used to people telling me I was hot."

Kassie just kept looking at him, but he turned his attention back to the road, which curved slightly through the grass-covered dunes just before the asphalt dumped out onto the sand by the pier. Her gaze made him feel uncomfortable, and he glanced at her again.

Now it seemed like she was glaring at him.

"I like you, Connor."

He felt a jolt but said nothing in response.

"Maybe you think I like somebody else?" she asked.

"I can't tell," he blurted out, then immediately regretted it. The road ended and the beach began. Horace Caldwell Pier was all lit up, stretching into the water. A few fishermen were out there. Connor turned right and headed down the beach.

Kassie looked out her window at The Dunes condominium.

"Sometimes I have fun with it, Connor. I've got this thing people want. They look at me and they think, 'Damn, I want to *fuck* her.'"

"Whoa," Connor said. "I mean, come on. That's kind of extreme."

Her gaze snapped back onto him. He suddenly felt false, even stupid, for having been dishonest out of politeness. He knew perfectly well that's what men—and maybe even some women—wanted from her. But he hadn't been honest enough to say so.

"Oh, yeah, Conner? You wouldn't like that? It sure felt like you wanted to do me at the Pod House. Maybe I'm wasting my time."

Connor couldn't believe what he was hearing.

"I'm not interested in wasting your time," he said.

His tires hit a lens of soft sand, the truck veered to the right, tossing Kassie onto him.

"Hey!" she yelled, laughing. "What are you trying to do, kill us?"

"Hey, yourself," he said. "You're supposed to be wearing a seatbelt."

Connor straightened the truck out, then turned to point at the surf, stopping a few yards from the water. The headlights lit up the first two sandbars of breakers.

Beach break for six million years—but how many times were the waves truly exceptional? How many times had tubes barreled across both sides of the peak, left and right, for thirty or forty yards, like they seemed to do almost every day on the North Shore?

Kassie put her hand on Connor's leg. They sat there looking at the Gulf.

Maybe she'll give me another chance, Connor thought. She'd thrown the bullshit she was sick of right out there in his face; after all the letters they'd written to each other talking about friendly, common interests, she wanted to see what he was made of. *But what if she thinks I don't have what it takes?*

Kassie liked how his thigh felt under her hand.

Still, she had doubts.

They rolled their windows down. She heard the Gulf's dull hiss, saw the waves sloshing. It was weak surf. Maybe she was just projecting a magnetism onto him that he didn't have. What good was having everything she wanted except the things she thought of in her most secret thoughts? What if he couldn't get her pulse up? She had been hoping that he would be the extra-smart lover she needed who also had guts—and the extreme lust she fantasized about.

Kassie felt him press his leg against hers. He smelled like restaurant and sweat, and a little bit like coconut sunscreen and surf wax. His leg pressure felt like some kind of heaven, smooth like cream. She started to feel herself getting hot.

Connor turned off the truck, then the lights. They sat longer than either one realized, until their eyes in the dark saw the sudden bursts of white foaming fluorescence with each breaking wave.

"Bioluminescence," Connor said.

Kassie turned to him in the dark. He, in turn, looked at her: She had a face too beautiful to believe, but there it was, right there, looking up at him. And it looked serious.

"I'm supposed to be home soon," she said. But she didn't move away from him.

"I wish you didn't, but I guess you might get in trouble if you don't."

Kassie said nothing.

Connor spoke again: "I want to go surfing with you tomorrow. I'm not letting that bastard Stamford get anywhere near you. I know that guy. He's been my friend for years. He's a total slut. He told me he was going to nail you, and it pissed me off. So I told him no. I said I was going to make you mine before you went home to Midland. It was a stupid bet. I did it just to provoke him—to piss him off."

"Wait. You told him you were going to make me yours?" Kassie asked.

"I just wanted to piss him off."

"You're saying you only wanted to piss him off?"

Connor didn't fall for it. He stayed cool.

"What do you think?" he asked.

"I think I want you to be the most dangerous one of them all."

———

Every day, crew boats ran in and out of Port Aransas harbor to the offshore rigs. Stamford would point at them from the south jetty, telling Connor how cool they were.

Fifty to sixty feet long, the high-powered boats were used to haul men and supplies out to the oil platforms and standpipes. The bridge was shoved up close on the bow, with the crew cabin stretching out behind, three to five windows on each side.

"That's where the roughnecks sit," Stamford said, pointing. "Three or four linoleum tables and bench seats in rows on port and starboard. See how the back deck is flat, with no railing? That's where they load all the heavy equipment—generators, pumps, big pieces of pipe, all the welding gear. There's no railing, because they need to use cranes to get goods on and off the boat. The railings would get in the way."

"Oh, yeah?" Connor said. "Who cares?"

Stamford laughed out loud and then said: "I do, you bastard."

Stamford had always liked all kinds of boats, ever since he was a small kid, but crew boats were extra-cool in his mind. They were sleek, loud, and fast. When his dad would take him fishing on the south jetty, he'd always watch the boats, but especially the crew boats, because they never seemed to slow down, no matter how high the swell was. He loved watching the boats launch from one swell and then plow into the next one, creating a huge crash of white water that would blow back across the entire length of the ship.

Stamford imagined how the pilot would be standing at the wheel, keeping pace with the rhythm, and getting tossed up and down with the heaving of the ship.

"Man," he said to Connor, "I gotta do that when I grow up."

"You are grown up, for Christ's sake," Connor answered. "You're grown up, and you're spending the night in jail."

That almost woke Stamford up, but not quite. He had passed out on the hard bunk of the police holding cell and had no idea where he was.

———

Connor had settled in next to Kassie. It felt good and right. It wasn't possible, but it was just like she had been the girl across the street who he'd grown up with, who had been into all the same geeky stuff he'd been into, who had watched the same TV shows, who had rooted for the same NFL teams—and then one day turned out to be the most beautiful woman he'd ever seen. He could smell her faint scent of perfume still, and it was intoxicating. He needed to move—do it now—so he turned his head and gently kissed the side of her neck.

She leaned her head to let him, and her body shivered with desire.

"I want to let you keep doing this," Kassie said, as Connor let his lips work down her neck and around toward the front of her body, heading down toward her cleavage. "But if you keep doing this, I'm going to lose it. I'll lose control."

Connor was hard as steel. He thought he was going to explode.

"I'm gonna lose it, too," he said, lifting himself up slightly to look at her as his hand stroked gently through her hair. He went to kiss her, but she pulled back very slightly.

He immediately backed off.

"I'm sorry," he said.

"No, Connor," Kassie said. "It's just that ... "

"Just that what?"

"I know it sounds stupid, but I want to go surfing with you tomorrow—and, well, my dad ... " she said, her voice trailing off.

"You're afraid of being grounded again?" he asked, grinning. "That would definitely ruin our fun tomorrow."

"Right," she said. "Besides, if we keep going like this there might be little Connors and Kassies running around on the beach next year."

She took his hand and placed it between her legs, which parted slightly.

Connor felt his heart jump, but she moved his hand away.

"I want it," she said. "I want you. But I'm afraid."

"I'm not afraid ... well ... I mean, that would be something, wouldn't it? Chasing kids around on the beach? You're making me delirious, Kassie. And you're trembling."

"Not because it's cold," she said.

Connor made himself grip the steering wheel with both hands.

"OK. I'm not letting go of this," he said, clenching his teeth with determination. "If I let go of this again, you'll be grounded—and if we don't want to be chasing little Kassies and Connors around the beach, I'd better drive you home."

Connor only took his hand off the steering wheel to turn the key and start the engine before putting it right back. Kassie adjusted her clothes but stayed close to him, sitting in the center of the truck's bench seat; Connor could feel her still trembling. He turned the headlights on, put his truck in reverse, backed away from the surf, and turned south.

They rode back to her condo in comfortable silence, shoulder to shoulder, her legs on one side of the floorboard gear shift, his legs on the other. Once they got to the Sea Isle condominiums, he pulled up to her condo unit, and she kissed him briefly on the cheek. He kept clutching the steering wheel, smiling at her. He wanted to say something to her—words wanted to come out of his mouth—but he clamped it shut. They weren't the right words right now, though he knew they were true.

"I'll see you at dawn," he said, looking at her through the passenger-side window.

"Yes, you will," she said. Their eyes lingered on each other for a moment, and she wanted to blurt out words that might be true. But she couldn't say them, not now, and maybe they weren't even really the right words. So she said goodnight and turned away, regretting that she had asked to be brought home—and, at the same time, afraid of being late.

She hurried up the stairs to the second floor, let herself in, relieved that her dad wasn't waiting up. She heard Connor's truck start and pull away, then went to her bedroom in the dark. She undressed quickly and got in bed, still shivering and trembling in fits and bouts.

Like a scared little girl, she thought. But she wasn't scared at all. For the first time, she felt herself fully a woman, fully adult, flirting with—and completely in charge of—her own destiny.

SEVEN

CONNOR DRIFTED in and out of sleep. He tried not to think about Kassie, but kept thinking about her anyway. He thought of Kassie under him, pulling him into her, then imagined Kassie was ignoring him at a party and flirting with other guys. He didn't want to think about that, so he imagined memories of spring break, when the island was overrun by college kids and high schoolers from across the state—and farther away, too.

Crowds surged over the beach, with cars parked door to door all the way down to the Beach Lodge. The drinking, music, and partying always pushed toward complete breakdown of law and order. Revelers wore baseball caps that sported a can of beer on each side with hoses into their mouths. They used vodka and tequila bongs to blast booze down their throats. Lewdness was a creed, impromptu wet T-shirt contests happened wherever and whenever, rock music blasted from countless pickup trucks, cars, and station wagons stuffed full with revelers. Sunscreen was unknown and in the wild nights, nudity and uncountable acts of sex were the norm.

Connor drifted between conscious remembrance and dream.

"God, this sucks," he said to Stamford while they stood at the end of Avenue G watching cars full of people roll past. "How will I ever find Kassie down here?"

"Are you crazy, dude?" Stamford said. "Who cares about her? Just look at all these carloads of hot chicks! We're in heaven, man!"

The overtaxed ferry system disgorged cars and trucks from the mainland, full of college-age men and women, rocking to AC/DC, Aerosmith, and Nazareth, or playing Peter Frampton, Boston, and Kiss full blast. Many more came barreling up the Island Road from Corpus.

"Well," Connor said, watching a Ford Bronco drive by with its top removed, filled with partying, bikini-clad women drinking beer from a keg hose, "I guess you have something of a point."

They had walked along the car line, moving much faster than the vehicles, with Stamford shouting out at girls, who shouted back at him.

Connor remembered encountering a row of overweight, sunburned frat guys who had set up lawn chairs on the beach right next to the cars inching by. They shouted ratings at women—"Eight!" "Five!" "Three!" "NINE!"—as spittle flew out of their frothing mouths.

"Look at those jerks," Connor had complained to Stamford. Connor hated their hubris and the gall it took someone as out of shape and plain as these beer-bellied, lobster-red, sunburned men to be shouting ratings at women. He wanted to go over and rip the signs out of their putrid hands and kick them out of their lawn chairs.

"Those guys rate less than zero," Stamford said matter-of-factly.

A truck had paused in front of the self-appointed judges, and they spotted a coed glugging from a fat can of Foster's, holding it with both hands as she tipped it back into her gullet.

"TEN!" they had yelled, holding up signs scrawled in magic marker with their highest mark.

The woman heard. She looked down at them with a look of raw fury.

"You fucking assholes!" she yelled, pointing at them.

The row of guys started hooting even louder. The woman sprang down off the back of the truck and ran straight down the line of guys, shaking her can of Foster's and spewing beer all over the lot of them. Several tumbled over backward, their aluminum chairs collapsing, while others jumped up and scrambled away. One fell on his face, and she threw her empty Foster's can at him. It bounced off his head, and everyone who saw it applauded.

Connor realized he was making out with a spring break girl in a Suburban. It had gotten dark. The girl was restless and stopped kissing him.

"You're not doing what you're supposed to be doing," she said, then grabbed one of his hands and put it firmly on her breast.

"There," she said.

Connor realized he must be dreaming, because this had actually happened to him a couple of years before, when he was a sophomore in high school. But before he could do what he was supposed to be doing, the car door was suddenly yanked open. Kassie stood there, glaring at them—*at him*—and the girl he was making out with vanished.

"Kassie, I can explain," he started to say, but Kassie slammed the door shut and vanished.

Connor bolted upright in his bed before realizing, to his great relief, that it was just a dream.

Come on, man, he thought to himself. *That was over the top. You need to chill the hell out about Kassie.*

But he didn't. He was just as worked up about her as he had been after he had dropped her off at her condo. Nothing seemed to help. He lay in bed, eyes wide open, until dawn spread her rosy fingers across the sky.

Time to get up. He had a date.

It was getting light, and Kassie hadn't slept well. Through the miniblinds, she saw the light of the approaching sunrise. She rolled over and squeezed her eyes shut, hoping for a little more sleep, but her thoughts wouldn't let her rest anymore. She felt a strong feeling inside her—a powerful reverberation of the feelings she'd experienced last night.

I don't get it, she thought. She'd gone parking before, and it had been exciting. But something different happened last night. She didn't want to say it, though. Instead, she tried to make the thoughts creeping into her head go away. She grabbed the other pillow on the bed and smashed it over her head.

"Go away," she said to the image of Connor in her head.

The thoughts wouldn't leave, though. Dancing with Connor, him holding her, pressing up against her naturally without being salacious. He simply felt warm, firm, and safe. She could still smell him on her hands. It was a surfer's smell: Mr. Zogs Sex Wax and coconut tanning oil—and the tequila taste when she'd kissed him. She hugged herself and thought of the beach last night, how natural it had felt sitting next to him and talking with him, like she felt around her mom or dad. Like it was the way it always had been. That was dangerous. She might say anything—or everything.

She tried to imagine Connor in the future with someone else. A brief image appeared in her head of Connor standing at the altar, reciting marriage vows to a woman—not her—and she wanted to shout "No!" before rushing down the aisle to grab his hand, lead him outside, and make an escape.

Don't be a moron, she thought. *Don't think of him with someone else. It's just proving what you already know.*

So she let her thoughts drift to where they really wanted to go.

It was him, she was pulling his face down to kiss her, her hand over him, feeling what he had. Reaching down for real, her hand slow across her neck, over her clavicle. It was easy to imagine in the dim light that it was Connor's warm hand on her breast, slowly working its way down over her belly. Smooth, firm, confident.

"Just stop," she muttered to herself, but it was hopeless.

She had a vision of Connor, lying on her, on the beach, in the sunshine. She could hear the sound of waves, felt him over her, a power stronger than either of them. It was a desire that rose like an oncoming line of swell, one wave after the next, smooth like rising walls of glass. He filled into her, then back out, over and over, each wave in the set bigger, until finally the last one rose high enough—and him inside—that the wave crested and folded over, crashing into whitewater flame. Her back arched suddenly, and she let out a soft cry of release.

"God," she said, panting, pressing her face into her pillow, "God, please let these things be true."

EIGHT

AT SUNUP, Connor got in his truck and drove down to the Ice Box, bought chocolate-covered mini-doughnuts and a Dr Pepper. He cracked open the can and slugged it.

"Good morning, Port Aransas," he said before stuffing a waxy mini-doughnut in his mouth.

Licking bad chocolate from his fingers, holding the cold drink between his legs, he gunned the truck and squealed onto Avenue G heading for the beach. At the crest of the hill, by his cottages, the sun refracted sharply through the wet dew of Gulf water on the windshield, blinding, like frozen frost—but it was morning saltwater dew instead. He turned on the wipers, but they just smeared the salty moisture into an opaque sheen. There was no wiper fluid; Connor never remembered to add any.

So he stuck his head out of his open door window to see.

Sunrise on the Texas coast was a colorful profusion: The Gulf hosted scattered thunderstorms, white-rimmed dark blue puffs with rays of gold gleaming all round, towering high, sunbeams dancing over dark waters. The tops of distant storms pulsed with flashes of lightning.

"Wow," he said aloud. "Maybe there will be some good waves today."

Avenue G ended, and his truck lurched through patches of soft sand that turned to hardpack by the water's edge. He got out and stared, chomping the last doughnut and washing it down with a final gulp of Dr Pepper.

The waves were a little less than waist-high, well-formed, and glassy.

What the hell, he thought. *Maybe even the surf gods want this to happen.*

He imagined Kassie screeching as the cool whitewater slapped against her belly, laughing, cursing, shivering. Her smile while looking right at him.

Connor got back in his truck, fired it up, headed south down the beach. He wasn't going to let Stamford take Kassie and ruin her for him. She was going to be his by the end of summer—or bust.

Bust, he figured. *It'll be a bust. She's too hot for me—way out of my league.*

And yet he knew in his head that his doubts weren't exactly supported by how Kassie was behaving, by the things she said—by how she had acted when she was with him. His head believed in Kassie, but his heart did not.

That morning, he'd known it was way too early to call someone on the phone, but he hadn't been able to stop himself. He'd dialed the number on the crumpled piece of paper she'd given him the night before with no fear. Even though it was so early, it felt like he was calling a best friend before an early morning surf session. The phone rang just once before he heard the receiver get snatched up.

"Hi," Kassie whispered. "Are you coming to get me?"

Her voice shot raw adrenaline into his heart. Everything about her was perfect, and everything had gone perfectly with her.

Don't psych yourself out, dumbass, he thought.

On the one hand, she had ditched Stamford at the party, then ditched him again after showing up with him at Pelican's. That had thrown Connor for a loop. But at Boxcar Billy's, she hadn't left with Stamford, nor had she climbed into Maxim's car. She'd asked *him* for a ride home.

He spit out the window of his truck onto the sand.

She's too hot for me, he said to himself again. *Too hot to handle.*

Every guy on the planet hit on her. They hit on her now, and they would hit on her in the future.

Christ. Would I want every jackass on the planet hitting on my wife?

Connor busted out laughing, then glanced at himself in the rearview mirror.

"Come on, man," he said. "Wife? Really?"

The truck jolted suddenly and noisily over a piece of driftwood, which banged hard against the bottom of his truck.

"Shit."

Connor looked in the rearview mirror at the bouncing, receding black log.

Kassie was a fox. Even women often stared at Kassie—sometimes unhappily, but mostly with envy, wonder, and appreciation. Or lust.

No, Connor thought. *Best to just be friends. Don't risk it.*

He'd be seared, flame-kissed, charbroiled, and left half-eaten on the plate. When she was bored with him, Kassie would head off with the latest Mr. Right Now, just like his mom had done to his dad.

To him.

"I won't win," Connor said aloud as he stared at the dark, glassy waves. "I can't, and I won't. But even if I did catch her, I couldn't keep her."

The smell of dead fish wafted through his window. He realized he'd passed his beach exit. He scanned the area for cops, then fishtailed a hard U-turn and drove off the beach onto asphalt, heading toward the Sea Isle condominiums.

In Stamford's drunken dream, the twin General Motors nine-hundred-and-fifty-horsepower diesels roared, spouting black smoke out of the stack just behind the bridge. It looked, and smelled, like raw power. A huge rooster tail of whitewater exploded behind the wide, flat stern of the crew boat.

It leapt forward, and Stamford almost fell down before grabbing one of the holds at the edge of the crew cabin. The boat was hauling ass in a matter of seconds. The wind snapped the flags, and the bow crashed hard into the oncoming swell, sending a massive spray all the way back to where he was. He let it hit him, and it almost knocked him loose from the handhold. The seawater drenched his clothes.

"Hell, yeah!" Stamford shouted at the sky, exuberant. This was his first day as a crew boat deckhand, and he couldn't wait to get home to tell Connor and his other buddies about it.

On either side of the boat, fifty yards away, the north and south jetties slid past in the early morning sunrise pink. The closer the crew boat got toward the end of the jetties, the heavier the swell became, the more the boat heaved up and down, the more it lurched into the swell. The bow spray was spectacular.

Stamford crab-walked over to the middle of the clear

deck, close to the main cabin hatch, and hands free, slowly stood up, balancing on the heaving deck like he was on a surfboard. Soon the boat passed the tips of the jetties, and he saw the dark-green swell bursting over the last few moss-covered granite blocks. He remembered that day long ago when a bunch of them were playing at the end of the south jetty, and Hilton had been taken by the sea. A huge rogue wave had rolled onto the end and snatched Hilton as it washed back out and he was caught by the rising follow-on wave, which was even bigger. They saw him flailing in a growing whitewater wall that peaked before forcefully throwing him back onto the jetty rocks. He'd ended up with just a scraped knee.

"Christ, you lucky bastard," Connor had said, as Hilton scrambled with them back along the gigantic square blocks of granite toward safety. "Your brains should be bashed out."

The crew boat had started launching and landing hard enough in the swell to make it difficult to stand without holding onto something—and then, when it turned southeast, a huge wedge of spray from the port side blew across Stamford, knocking him off balance and pushing him over toward the starboard gunwale. He fell to one knee to keep from going completely over the side.

"Shit," he said, scrambling like Hilton had done back to safety. Thoroughly soaked, Stamford opened the heavy crew cabin hatch and went in, dripping water all over the linoleum floor. A couple of roughnecks going out to the rig grinned at him.

"You just made me lose ten bucks, damn it," said one of them. "I bet you'd get blown overboard."

"Pay up, man," his buddy said.

"After we get back in from our rotation," the roughneck replied.

"I wasn't even close to being knocked overboard," Stamford said, lurching toward them.

Both men turned and eyed him briefly, then looked at each other and laughed.

"A newbie," one said.

The engine noise changed to a knocking sound, clanging like something was breaking. Stamford might be a newbie, but he knew the sound of breaking engine metal. The engines were seriously knocking and clanging, louder and louder—until Stamford realized it wasn't an engine at all. When he opened his eyes, he saw Clint, the Port Aransas police sergeant, standing outside the cell, grinning and whacking the cell bars with his billy club.

"Wake up, jackass," Clint said. "Time to get home. You're sober enough. I'll give you a ride back over to your truck at Boxcar Billy's."

Stamford was confused. His head hurt.

"What the hell?" he asked, blinking and looking around, not understanding where he was.

Seeing this, Clint shook his head.

"You got arrested last night, jackass," he told Stamford.

"Arrested? What for?"

"Public intoxication, drinking alcohol in an illegal location, resisting arrest—and just generally being your sweet, loveable self."

Clint had been a senior in high school when Stamford was in seventh grade. They'd known each other most of their lives.

Stamford sat up. It stank like sweat and vomit in the cell. Grime and sludge caked the corners. He grabbed his head with both hands and moaned, his skull aching with hangover.

"Jeez," he said. "I had no idea I was such an outlaw."

"You smarted off to the newbie," Clint said, absently

inspecting the tip of his billy club. "He don't know you from Adam, and you pissed him off with your high-dollar swagger."

"The newbies," Stamford muttered. "Got to watch over the newbies. They don't know how powerful the water can be."

Clint raised an eyebrow, having no idea what Stamford meant.

"Anyway," Clint said, purposefully banging the cell bars really hard with the club so that Stamford winced, "I'll get the charges dropped if you bring me a case of steaks and a couple of sixers."

NINE

CONNOR WATCHED as Kassie came out of her condo's second-floor unit and skipped down the flights of steps carrying a cloth beach bag.

At the truck she looked briefly at the surfboard in the bed, then opened the door and got in.

"I saw you pull up," she said, smiling. She set the bag down then leaned over and kissed his cheek. "I'm excited. I've always wanted to learn how to surf."

"Yeah!" Connor said. "It's a good day for it, too. Clean and waist-high."

Kassie had set her bag down between them on the bench seat and had already put her seatbelt on.

"Let's go!" she said.

"Well all right, then."

Connor started the truck, shoved a cassette tape he'd mixed into the stereo, and they drove off. He almost cringed when he heard the song "Bobby Brown" by Frank Zappa, but Kassie hooted and busted out singing the lyrics.

"I can't believe you like Zappa, too," she said.

Good God, I'm in love with her, Connor thought. She was incredible. Even in Playboy or Penthouse, he'd never seen a woman as hot as Kassie. It was hard for him to pretend he wasn't utterly smitten.

For God's sake, dude, why would you pretend about that when you've never wanted a girl as bad as you want her?

He pretended anyway.

They drove south on Eleventh Street. He wanted to go far enough south to where it was unlikely that any of the surf-shop dudes would be driving past, particularly Stamford—who, he hoped, was still locked up in the Port Aransas jail.

After the Zappa song finished, he reached the access road and turned left. Now AC/DC's "Hell Ain't a Bad Place to Be" was playing. Again, Kassie was bopping to the music and singing along.

Connor laughed.

"What?" she asked.

"I thought you were Catholic, and all that."

She grinned.

"So we're not going to the pier?" she asked. "I thought you said the waves were better at the pier."

"Huh? Well, no. Better down here so we won't be bothered."

"Good. I don't want any Kevins showing up."

She flashed her eyes at him, wanting him to know she liked the idea of having him to herself.

"Besides," she added, "I don't want anyone watching me kook out. I don't want anyone around watching if things get out of control."

Connor looked at her, thinking about what she meant, but he sidestepped with a question.

"Did you just say, 'kook out?' " Connor said. "How do you know that word?"

"Come on," she said. "Surf magazines, of course—and hanging around the North Shore watching the scene."

When they got to the beach, the sun was sandwiched between the distant tops of thunderstorms. Those storms were driving in small sets of lined-up waves.

Connor pulled up near the water's edge and parked.

"Doesn't look like much," Kassie said, raising her eyebrows.

"Yeah, it never does," he said. "But it'll surprise you once you get out to the third bar. Tide's going out, so it'll probably steepen the waves."

"The third bar? Do we have to go that far out?" Kassie said, sounding worried.

The sudden concern startled Connor. He hadn't thought about it.

"I mean, no," he said. "But it's not that deep out there. Where the waves break, it's maybe waist- or chest-deep."

Kassie stared out the window, biting her lower lip.

"Shoot," she said, turning to Connor with bright, happy eyes. "Let's do this!"

Connor got his Weber Winger out of the back of his truck. He'd found it at Geri's Surfboard Shop five years ago. It was his first surfboard, a fish design by Dewey Weber. It originally had sharp little fiberglass winglets that stuck out horizontally at the tail, supposedly to keep the board from spinning out during a hard turn. But all they seemed to do for Connor was cut his knees, so he'd jerked them out.

"This board was pretty good for me to learn on," he told Kassie, "so I figure it'll be a good one for you to learn on, too."

"Okay," she said. "Why don't you go down to the water while I change?"

"Sure," Connor said.

She was wearing a T-shirt and shorts. Now he wondered what was in the bag.

"My bikini's in my bag," she said, answering the question in his mind. "I'll have to dump my clothes, so don't cheat and look back at me."

"Who, me?" he asked. "A Peeping Tom? What kind of perv do you take me for?"

"Well the first song on your cassette was 'Bobby Brown.'"

Connor smirked.

"Okay," he said. "Maybe I am a little perverted."

Kassie smiled a bit devilishly, raised one eyebrow a tad.

Good God, there's nothing about her that isn't burning hot, Connor thought.

He lingered.

"Well?" she asked.

"Um. Oh, yeah. I'm supposed to go to the water. I'll wax the board."

"That's right, Connor," she said. "Over by the water. I mean, I'm not exactly going to do a striptease for you—at least not right now. You promised to teach me how to surf. So get going!"

Connor's heart was pumping hard. He turned and walked to the water without looking back. He put the board down near the water and started waxing it. No way he was going to look back at the truck, even though he wanted to. He imagined Kassie taking her shorts off, then her T-shirt, letting them drop to the ground, then walking over to him with nothing on, taking him by the hand.

"Stop," he said aloud to himself.

"Stop what?" Kassie said.

Startled, Connor looked up. Kassie stood above him, brown in the rising sun, wearing a black bikini, puka shell necklace, and a thin leather anklet on her left foot.

"Nothing," he said, grinning, as he continued to wax the board.

She liked looking down at Connor's back, liked seeing his strong back muscles—*like a Greek god,* she thought—how square his shoulders were, how his triceps stood out as he moved the surf wax over the board, how striking his eyes were when he looked up at her.

While Kassie ogled him, she quickly put her hair into a ponytail. The breaking waves made a steady washing sound, the effect of thousands of waves constantly arriving up and down the shoreline. It was totally different than the North Shore—maybe like Mission Beach at San Diego, but smaller. Much smaller, but also much warmer.

"That's a pretty small board," she remarked.

"It works well in waves this size," Connor responded automatically. But something about her statement—the tone of voice she used—left him a little confused. She sounded like she knew exactly what she was talking about, but he believed she'd never really surfed much before. So he said nothing and scrubbed on more wax.

"What kind of wax is that?" she asked.

"Mr. Zog's Sex Wax," he answered, then added: Wait a second—I thought you hadn't surfed before."

Kassie laughed.

"Sex Wax? Hmm. "Bobby Brown," "Hell Ain't a Bad Place to Be," and now Sex Wax. Are you trying to tell me something, Connor?"

He was suddenly embarrassed.

"Oh, jeez," he said. "Like I said, I'm sorry. I forgot what was on the tape. I just pushed it in."

"You just pushed it in," she said. "Well, I never heard of Sex Wax. What's it for?"

"Surf wax keeps your feet from sliding off the surfboard. Here, check it out."

Connor picked up the board and turned the top toward her so she could touch it.

"See? You can't slide your finger over it so easy," he said. "But check this out."

He flipped the unwaxed bottom side of the surfboard to face her, and she stroked her fingers over the bottom.

"You couldn't stand on an unwaxed fiberglass board," he explained. "You couldn't even get on it, because it's crazy slick when it gets wet."

Kassie smirked and gave him a sideways glance.

"You're into double entendres," she said.

"What's double on ... I mean, who is Tondra?" Connor asked, confused.

"You don't know Tondra?" Kassie replied, laughing.

"No. Um ... maybe I should?"

Kassie tried to get hold of herself, but she felt more and more like taking the surfboard out of this hot guy's hands and making out with him right here on the beach. He was just what she wanted, and she knew it. There was no pretending otherwise. Best to have him—have him right now—and then maybe he could show her how to surf.

"Okay Connor," she said, trying to check her emotions. She paused, swallowing a sudden ache in her throat, "so now what?"

"Now we go surfing," he said.

He slung the board under his arm, and they marched out through the tiny wavelets lapping the sand, splashing then ankle-deep, thigh deep—and that's when the short blasts of water started to shock them with cold. Halfway out, Kassie was jumping and squealing as the waves lapped over her belly, just like Connor had imagined she would.

"Damn it!" she exclaimed. "This water's cold!"

"Don't worry," Connor replied. "You'll warm up."

They kept wading, and for the moment Connor and Kassie said nothing more, listening instead to the waves, and the dull sound of the breaking surf. The water appeared like a silvery mirror when the sun glanced off it, then as a dark, clear green. A couple of mullet flew out of the water near the second bar, and a pelican came flying across at wave height, skimming for fish.

"Man, I love those," Kassie said.

"They're pretty awesome," Connor said. "Maybe we'll get lucky, and a bottlenose dolphin will come check us out."

"What? Aren't those dangerous?"

"Nah. We want them around as much as possible. When you see one up close, it's just incredible. They're so much bigger than they look from shore."

Soon they were past the first bar, and the water was getting up to be chest deep.

"All right," Connor said. "Get on the board. Just lay on it, and I'll push you out farther. It gets a little deep here."

"How do I do it?"

Connor explained, and she did it just like he said, but Kassie had all kinds of trouble balancing.

"Whoa!" she said, "this thing's uncontrollable!" Then she laughed again.

But Kassie managed to position herself a little better on the board, and Connor pulled her out to the second bar. The water quickly got shallow, and he told Kassie to get off and walk.

"Just follow me, and do what I do," Connor said to her. "We'll hop up over the small waves and dive under the bigger ones."

"OK."

In a minute or two, they got past where the waves were breaking.

"That was a lot harder than I thought it would be," Kassie said. "The waves aren't big, but they shove you all over the place."

"Yeah," Connor said. "We'll rest and let a couple sets pass if you're tired."

"Naw, let's do this!"

"Then get on the board like you did before," he said. "Once you're on, I'll turn the board around for you—and when a smaller wave comes, I'll push you into it."

"OK."

Kassie struggled onto the board, her legs flopping off to the side without any coordination, and her balance completely off. Her movements rocked the board clumsily, first from side to side, then dunking the nose, then being a little too far to the back. She laughed the whole time.

"Oh, my God, this is hard!"

"You'll get the hang of it."

As Connor moved the board into position, he tried not to look at every inch of her, but her body was absolutely perfect. Her bronzed skin, her amazing back muscles, with the water droplets sparkling, and the dimples just over her butt— all of it was about to make Connor lose control of himself and do something he thought would ruin everything.

A set passed, and then a smaller wave appeared. It was peaking up just right.

"I see one coming," he yelled. "Are you ready?"

"No!" Kassie shouted with fake alarm.

"You're going anyway," Connor said.

The wave walled up. It looked perfect, and Connor heaved as hard as he could just as the wave was passing. It had jacked up suddenly, making Connor think for sure that

Kassie and the board were going to nosedive straight down into the sand bar. The takeoff was too late. He clenched his teeth, expecting disaster.

Then Connor watched in absolute shock as Kassie snapped to her feet and turned regular-foot frontside on the wave. She flew down the line, pumping the board up and down as the wave broke right behind her. His jaw dropped when the wave peaked up again twenty yards down, and she flicked the board in an off-the-lip so vertical that Connor could see the whole front half of the board pointing at the sky —and then it was gone. She'd whipped the board around instantly, then landed it solid.

Kassie stood relaxed over the spent wave, unwinding the tension before kicking out.

Connor's mouth remained open.

She saw his expression and laughed before dropping into paddling position. She stroked hard back out to where he was, grinning broadly, her body covered with shimmering water droplets and her lean, rippling muscles pulling her powerfully through the water. The surfboard slapped up and down over the waves, and her posture was that of someone who'd been surfing for years.

Kassie stopped next to him and sat up on the board, its blunt nose pointing skyward. She raised both hands behind her head, pulled her ponytail around, and draped it down over the front of her shoulder.

"Well," she said, "how about that shit?"

TEN

BACK AT KASSIE'S CONDO, Connor slammed the Lone Star she gave him, then threw himself on the couch, laughing. He still couldn't believe it. They had spent several hours trading out the board and catching waves, trying to one-up each other, and in the end the winner was obvious: Kassie Hernandez.

"I can't believe how good you can surf," he said. "I mean, a switch-foot roundhouse cutback? That actually pissed me off. I'm not sure I can like you anymore."

"Hey, watch your language," Kassie said. "If my mom heard you say 'pissed off,' she'd blow a gasket!"

"Ah, but we're alone."

"That's right," she said, and her heart beat a little bit faster. Her parents had left a note that they'd gone to Corpus Christi for some shopping at Padre Staples Mall.

Kassie took two more Lone Stars from the fridge before walking over to Connor. She had decided it didn't taste so bad after all, and at least it seemed to help her get a buzz on. She saw he was watching her every move, and she liked that.

She put the cold beers on the coffee table, then stepped up onto the couch, put one leg across Connor's lap, and lowered herself slowly straight down, straddling him. His expression changed, and she leaned in to kiss him.

Connor's heart jumped; he put his hands on her, letting them move down her body before coming to rest on the cheeks he'd been lusting after all morning. He held them firmly, and she moved slowly against his lap.

Then she stopped suddenly and pulled back, looking at him.

"That was the most fun I've had surfing in a long time," she said.

Connor leaned in to kiss her, but she pushed him back.

"Not yet," she said.

"I don't want to talk," Connor said, trying to lean forward to kiss her again.

She pressed him back again, but only just.

"It'll be better this way," she said, pressing her hips into him again. She felt hot down there as her hand touched his face. "I mean, don't you want to talk about our surfing anymore? I thought you loved surfing."

"You were hogging up the board almost the whole time," he said, laughing. "But I never got tired of watching you."

Her lips parted slightly.

"I saw you watching me," she said. "I've been landlocked. I had needs. That squirrely board surprised me, though. It almost did the job."

"Almost?"

Connor knew she was a better surfer than he was. He thought it strange that it didn't bother him. With everyone else, he was always trying to gauge who was best, and how he stacked up. When she was sitting on his lap, surfing didn't matter.

Out of the blue, Kassie bluntly asked: "Connor, what are you going to do with the rest of your life?"

"Uh," he said, taken off guard. "Hmm. I mean, I've got my little aspirations to be a famous marine biologist who does breakthrough research with bottlenose dolphins."

"Flipper?"

"That's right, Flipper. My buddy Franklin's dad is the director at the Marine Science Institute here in Port Aransas. We go over there all the time to play pool and shuffleboard."

"What have pool and shuffleboard got to do with dolphins?" Kassie asked, amused.

"Nothing. But Franklin's dad likes me, and his dad is an expert on large marine mammals. He studies them. He told me he wants me to go to UT Austin and study marine biology —do some internships with him, and then a masters. You know what?"

"What?"

"I want to research why dolphins like to surf."

"That's a thing you can research?"

"Well," Connor said, a bit defensively, "Franklin's dad thought it was a cool idea."

Kassie felt him straining in his shorts, making her want to lie down with him and pull him on top of her. It was like a delirium. She sucked air in audibly, closed her eyes briefly and pushed back on him.

Connor put his hands on her arms.

"Kassie ... "

"What?"

"Right now, I just want what's sitting on top of me to be true for the rest of my life."

Kassie felt a jolt go through her, and an ache began in her throat. She leaned over him, her long brown hair framing his face on either side, his dark eyes looking up at her, filled with desire.

She had to have him. Now, right now. She pressed her hips into his lap, rubbing firmly up and down against his hardness, kissing his lips, his face, his neck.

The heat between her legs was making him crazy. Their hands started pulling clumsily at clothing, but before she had his T-shirt off, they heard loud footsteps stamping up the stairs—Kassie's mom and dad were bickering outside as a key was inserted into the door.

"Yes, you did say that, Mike Hernandez," her mom said, pausing as the door was open just a crack. "Why don't you just admit it and apologize so we can be done with this?"

Then the door swung open, too far, banging against the wall.

"Shit," her mom blurted. Then she saw Kassie and Connor, faces cast with strained smiles, hands folded in their laps. They were sitting on opposite ends of the couch.

"Oh," Kassie's mom said, confused, holding a shopping bag from the mall in Corpus. Then she seemed to snap out of it and put the bag on the kitchen table before reflexively straightening her dress.

"I didn't know you had company, Kassie. Excuse my French, young man, I ... "

"Your mom was being mad at me," Kassie's dad said, stepping into the condo. He walked past Kassie's mom and stopped, standing rather tall.

"So," he said as he looked at Connor, "I'm Mike Hernandez. And you?"

"Connor," blurted Connor and Kassie at the same time.

Kassie's dad let the awkward silence fan out across the whole room, saying nothing.

"Uh, Connor O'Reilly, sir," Connor added, nervously.

Connor knew he was supposed to stand up and go shake Mr. Hernandez's hand, but he couldn't get up off the couch. A copy of *Surfer* magazine he'd slapped over his lap hid why.

"So," Kassie's dad said, his eyes glittering, "I guess y'all were having a nice chat."

"Well, we were talking about surfing, Dad," Kassie said.

"I see. And chatting on completely *opposite* sides of the sofa," he said, gesturing with his hand. "That's quite admirable, Connor."

"Dad!"

Kassie's mom walked into the living room and stood by the coffee table. She looked first at Connor, then at Kassie, then the length of couch between them. The beer cans, too. She raised an eyebrow.

"I'm tired," Kassie's mom said. "You'll have to excuse me, Connor. I'm going to lay down for a bit. This coastal heat is murder."

She turned and walked away to her bedroom.

Kassie's dad followed his wife, but not before looking over his shoulder at them, smirking.

"I think they might have been smooching, honey," he said, pretending to talk low enough so that Kassie and Connor wouldn't hear him.

"Dad!"

Kassie's cheeks flushed with embarrassment. Connor sat, smiling as best he could, still covering his lap with the magazine, which had Gerry Lopez on the cover standing tall in a monster Banzai Pipeline tube.

ELEVEN

STAMFORD PULLED up to the surf shop and parked his truck, got out, and went inside.

Maxim looked up from some papers on the counter when he came in.

"Well, well," he said with a grin. "Our little felon."

"Ah, screw that," Stamford said. "I bought my way out of that one with a couple of cases of steaks from the boat. Never should have been taken in to begin with, Clint says."

"That's not what Clint told us," Sandi said, smirking.

"Whatever," Stamford said. "I'm a free man again."

"What do you hear from Kassie?" Maxim asked.

"Can't say I want to hear anything from that know-it-all smart ass. I have zero interest. I want my night back from that mess."

"She seems pretty hot to me," Maxim said. "Smart, too."

"You can have her."

"Yeah," Sandi added. "Why don't you see if you can bring her home to me, baby—if you think you can."

Maxim laughed.

"Is that a challenge?" he asked.

"Sure," Sandi said..

"It'll never happen," Stamford said. "She's too highfalutin for plain people like us. I mean, she's going to school in L.A.!"

"San Diego," Sandi said, frowning.

"Whatever," Stamford said. "Kassie will talk moon landing nonsense and airplane bullshit, solve impossible math problems to show off, and you'll want her gone before anything even gets going."

"Then I'll be a perfect student for *Madam Professor*," Maxim said with a grin. "You know Connor took her home the other night when you got dragged off to jail, right?"

"He can have her."

"Oh, I understand, dude. Rejection's hard. Not that I have much experience with it."

"I'll wager a hundred bucks you won't get anywhere with her, Maxim. If the expert can't have none, the novice sure won't."

Sandi laughed.

"Stamford, you're strokin' it five times a day," Maxim said.

Everyone in the shop laughed at that. But Maxim took Stamford's bet.

"Not like I need any extra motivation with Kassie," he said, adjusting his nuts through his white linen pants.

"You should put a shirt on, Maxim," Stamford said. "The only topless one I want to see in here is Sandi."

Kassie heard voices, but even with bright light the outlines were unclear. Not the voice, which was definitely her Uncle

Alan, talking about how he wouldn't pay for her to study astronomy—or especially engineering. His face came into sharp focus, leaning into hers: *"Not for girls."*

Fear—or maybe anger—made her want to turn away from him and find her dad. But she couldn't move her head or her body. She seemed to be completely restrained, even though nothing was holding on to her. It was like she was a statue.

"What's good enough for your Aunt Brenda is damn well good enough for you" her uncle said.

Then Aunt Brenda showed up. Naked. Kassie tried to turn away again, but her head wouldn't move. Then her aunt, in the magic way of dreams, suddenly was wearing a bra and panties, looking at least twelve months pregnant. Her belly appeared to be three feet across, and her stick arms and legs made her look like a weird cartoon.

"See this?" her uncle loudly asked as he ran his hand over Brenda's belly. "It's a baby, honey. It's a baby your Aunt Brenda has inside of her. See, I sell the cars, and she makes the babies. That's how it works."

"Kassie!" she heard her mom shout from somewhere out of sight.

Kassie then saw her hand writing the first letter she'd ever sent to Connor the year before. She had been completely honest, listing all the things she really wanted to do in life—all the things that weren't on her uncle's list of things women were allowed to do.

Her mom kept asking the same question. Insistent. Louder and louder. It was getting really annoying.

"Mom, for God's sake, what is it?"

The worst were the hyper-flirtatious dumbasses. She had to deal with them nearly every time she went out the door. *The door,* she thought, as she heard someone talking about buying groceries. It was that kind of shallow bullshit all the time.

But Connor had somehow walked right past all that, sat down, and simply started talking real shit to her. No meaningless jokes or drivel, just things they both felt real about. It had blown her away.

"I said, what do you want from the store, Kassie?"

"I want what's sitting on me to be true for the rest of my life."

Her mom didn't answer for a moment. Then Kassie felt her mom gently shaking her shoulder.

"Honey, that doesn't make any sense," her mom said. "Now wake up. I asked what you wanted from the store."

Kassie opened her eyes. Her mom was looking at her, a quizzical expression on her face.

"I'm going to the store," her mom said. "We're not eating out tonight. Dad and I are sick of all the restaurants already, so I'm gonna make something."

"Spaghetti?" Kassie asked, still confused.

Connor had talked with her about science, engineering, space—just like her dad. But Uncle Alan just stared at her over his newspaper.

"Not for girls," he said, then looked back down at his paper.

"So spaghetti and salad, and I'll get some ground beef and crackers," Kassie's mom said, looking at her list. "Lots of tomatoes, too. And garlic. We can make some meatballs! What else?"

Her dad, sitting in the sofa seat next to the couch, lowered his paper, a thoughtful look on his face. Of course it hadn't been Uncle Alan; she'd been dreaming.

"Wine," her dad said. "Not any of that Aldo Cella crap, either."

Kassie pushed herself up on her elbows. She had that bad taste of sleep in her mouth.

"Hey, how long have I been on the couch?" she asked.

"Two hours," her dad said. "I guess you surfed yourself out."

"Kassie, you never answered me," her mom said. "Anything you want?"

Connor, Kassie thought. *I want Connor on top of me. Right now.*

"I dunno, Ma. I guess wine."

"You guys are awful," her mom said as she grabbed her purse and headed for the door. "All right, I'm outta here. Be back in a few."

Then she paused.

"So, how was your 'surf lesson' today, Kassie?" her mom asked. "I can't believe you fooled that boy. What's his name again?"

"Connor."

"Right. What'd he say about your surfing? Did he think your practical joke was funny?"

"He thought I was the most perfect girl ever, Mom. He wants me to be with him for the rest of his life."

"Hmm. Yeah, no doubt. That's why y'all were sitting on opposite sides of the couch, huh? Honestly, I don't know whether he—or any other man—will ever make the grade, not to mention be able to match your valedictorian accomplishment and scholarship awards."

"What-*ever*, Mom," Kassie said, rolling her eyes.

Still, it felt good to be praised for being her school's valedictorian. That had been one hard haul to the top.

Her mom closed the door behind her, and Kassie heard flip-flops descending the stairs. Then she laid back on the couch and closed her eyes, thinking of Connor, and of all the good things he was. Then she thought about the bad things, about her uncle, and all the things he said were right but she knew in her heart were wrong. Those things made her feel she was going to be cheated. Her father turned a page of the paper, and it rustled. Pretty soon, she was almost dreaming again.

TWELVE

KASSIE WAS READING in her room when the phone rang. Her mom answered, said something muted. Then she heard mom coming toward her room. The door cracked open and she saw her mom's face

"It's that boy—what's his name?— the one who you were making out with the other day."

"Mom, that joke's getting a little old."

"Well, he wants to know if you're here or not."

Kassie's pulse quickened.

"Tell him I'll call right back, Mom," Kassie said, "and make sure and get his number."

"Get out of bed and get the number yourself, or I'll tell him you never want to see him again."

"Can't you just help a girl out, Mom?"

Her mom raised an eyebrow in reply.

Kassie hopped out of bed and went to the condo's living room, her mom close behind. Kassie picked up the receiver and glared at her mom, making a gesture with her hand and tilting her head toward her mom's room—signals for her to go away. Kassie's mom played dumb, so Kassie covered the mouthpiece and hissed, "I need some privacy, Mom."

Her mom rolled her eyes and stalked off. Kassie waited until she had gone into her own room and closed the door behind her.

"Hello?"

"Hey, it's Connor."

"Hi."

Connor heard a warmth in her simple reply, and it made him relax a little, even though he wasn't as tense as he used to be with her. Normally he would be sweating bullets talking to a girl as hot as Kassie—but, for some reason, he just wasn't with her.

"Let's go to Corpus," he said. "I want to take you to eat, then maybe catch a movie."

"Oh yeah? What movie?"

"*Free Ride.*"

"Shit. *Free Ride's* here?"

"Yeah, we gotta see it," Connor said. "But first I'm going to wine and dine you."

"Who, me?"

"Yeah, you."

"Well, I mean, it is *Free Ride* we're talking about. For that, anything, y'know?"

"The movie starts at eight-thirty," Connor told her. "I'll pick you up around six."

Kassie noted with pleasure that it wasn't a question.

"Come by earlier if you want," she said. "I mean, we could have a drink before dinner."

"I want to be there right now."

"No one's stopping you."

"I'll be there in two minutes."

"Wait," Kassie said, laughing. "I need an hour."

The shower water felt good. Even though it was hot outside in late summer, the condo's AC was always set super low, and with the tight feeling her skin still had from being in the sun most of the morning yesterday, the pulsing water relaxed her. She washed herself and enjoyed the sensual feeling of the soap sliding around. It was easy to get distracted and a fantasy flashed through her mind: Connor, naked, pulling the glass door open and getting in the shower with her, saying nothing, embracing her, pressing a strong hardness against her, his hands roving over her body, his mouth kissing hers, her melting in his embrace and opening for him.

There was a rapping on the bathroom door that brought her to her senses.

"Kassie, we're going out to eat," she heard her dad say in a raised voice. "I want you straight home after the movie, OK?"

"OK, Dad," she said.

Then the water pulsed over her again, and she felt her breasts, her nipples, which had gotten hard as she'd touched them thinking of Connor.

She shuddered and pushed those thoughts out of her head.

It seemed like Connor had what she wanted: Looks, smarts, a strong physique, and a brash wicked streak that was laser-focused on her. Just her. He wanted her bad, even if she were starting at UC San Diego in January. And she wanted him, even if they never saw each other after this summer. But nevermore wasn't an outcome she wanted.

Do I really want a long-distance relationship when I go to school? she wondered.

It was very likely she'd never see him again once she left for California.

I'll do him anyway, she thought as she touched herself again, but then stopped before she put herself over the edge.

She turned off the water and got out of the shower, grabbed a towel, dried off.

Maybe having a long-distance boyfriend was exactly what she needed to keep her out of trouble at school. His hands on her could only be imaginary if he were far away in Texas. No risk of pregnancy that way, and all she knew for sure was that she couldn't give up on her plan for school. Not for a guy—even for one as good as Connor O'Reilly.

"God," she pleaded, looking up at the ceiling, "why is this so hard?"

THIRTEEN

CONNOR PACED BACK and forth in his room, listening to the Kiss album *Dressed To Kill*. He needed every scrap of mojo he could muster. He was determined not to screw up with Kassie like Stamford had, even though he knew that, rationally, it was a completely ridiculous concern. But to his inexperienced, virgin self, there was always some measure of doubt.

He'd always had doubt with girls, but when he was with Kassie a mysterious force took over. No other girl had ever made the animal inside of him speak so plainly. What aggravated him most was that, when Kassie wasn't around, his internal warrior wasn't, either. In those moments, abandoned by vigor and forcefulness, he felt lame.

This is idiotic, he thought.

His feelings made him think of his mom. One morning Connor had come out of his room at breakfast. His dad was in the kitchen with a beer in his hand.

"She's gone," Connor's dad had told him.

"What do you mean?"

"I mean, she left us."

Connor had remained silent for a moment.

"She left me for Gene Stamford," his dad said. "They skipped town."

"Gene Stamford?"

Connor was floored.

"You mean Stamford's uncle, the minister guy?"

"They've been having an affair," his dad said as he took a swig of beer. "I suspected it. I figured it was just one more of her uncontrollable wild flings. I told her I wouldn't put up with it anymore. I told her this wasn't the sixties, and we had a kid, so she needed to get hold of herself."

Connor had only been peripherally aware of Stamford's uncle. Stamford didn't like to talk about Gene because his uncle was a minister. Connor's buddy Wilkins sang in Gene's church choir every Wednesday night and Sunday morning. Wilkins raved about how cool Stamford's uncle was, saying: "He even smokes weed!"

There was more to it than that, though. Connor's mom had been trying to get his dad to let her go back to school, because she wanted an art degree. There had been big fights, a lot of yelling, with epic screaming matches when Connor was a freshman in high school. He hated hearing his parents fight; to him, it mostly seemed like they consisted of his dad berating his mom.

At the time, he'd thought maybe it would be best if his parents split up—but, after they had, he didn't like it at all.

His dad had tried to downplay the effect of Connor's mom leaving with another man, but it became obvious over time that it was a powerful poison that wasn't easily remedied.

In the end, no matter how angry Connor was about his mom leaving, he missed her terribly.

Connor put the bad memory out of his mind by recalling how Kassie had executed two off-the-lips in a row the day before, causing a fan of spray to rise, beautiful glitters across the clear, greenish water, gems shimmering for a scant moment against the azure sky.

No surfer girl he knew had ever surfed like her, or looked like her, and it made his heart pump faster.

Finally, his digital clock showed it was 5 p.m., and he told himself to be nonchalant and confident when he picked her up, not overeager. He walked out of his room, saw his dad sitting on the sofa, cable news on the TV, reading a *Soldier of Fortune* magazine. Connor was a little worried about the dark turn his dad had taken since his mom had left them. He had once seen half a page that had been cut out of an ad that said, "Buy A Bullet. Kill A Communist."

"Dad, I'm going to Corpus for dinner and a surf movie."

His dad looked up over his reading glasses.

"Date?" he asked, raising his eyebrows.

"Date," Connor answered.

"Well, I hope she's a good one. Pretty, smart—and true."

Connor smiled.

"She's smart as hell, Dad, and the best surfer I've ever seen."

"Is she pretty?"

Connor grimaced.

"Maybe a little too pretty," he answered. "Every dude on the planet is after her."

———

Connor knew it was good when he didn't even have to get out of his car. Kassie practically sprinted down the stairs from the second-floor condo. She was smiling, her purse awhirl as she grabbed the door handle and jumped in. Immediately she leaned over and kissed Connor on the cheek to make sure things started off right.

"I can't believe we're going to see *Free Ride!*" she said.

"Yeah. It's supposed to be incredible."

"I read about it in *Surfer*," Kassie said.

"Well, I read about it in *Surfing*," Connor replied as he turned around and started backing his dad's black Cutlass Supreme out of the parking spot. "Everyone knows *Surfing* is better."

Kassie laughed.

"You're starting shit with me already?" she asked. "I can't believe it. I shouldn't have kissed you when I got in. It's made you all cocky."

Connor mashed the brakes, and Kassie whooped as she lurched backward. Connor was on her instantly, kissing her hard—but only for a moment.

"There," he said. "That's cocky if you want cocky."

He had delivered what he thought was his first conscious double entendre, and he wondered if she had noticed it.

"Well," she said, "I think that had a positive effect."

She wiggled in her seat, adjusting her shorts and straightening her blouse, then smoothed it back down over her flat tummy before flashing a smile at Connor.

"Let's just try and behave ourselves," she said. "Otherwise, we might never make it to the movie tonight."

A burst of hot desire ripped through Connor. They looked at each other intensely.

"Are your parents home?" he asked. "I could stay right here and forget all that other stuff."

Kassie felt it: He had just penetrated through the veneer.

"I know," she said darkly, suppressing a tremble. "But let's drive to Corpus anyway. *Free Ride* is worth the trouble

—and you never know when surf films will quit circulating."

Dinner had been one long flirtation, with both Connor and Kassie sipping on frozen margaritas while eating chips, salsa, queso, and enchiladas. It seemed like they couldn't run out of things to talk about. When they walked back out to the car, she took Connor's hand and held it. He had to use every bit of willpower he had to keep from pressing her against the Cutlass and making out with her—then his willpower vanished, and he did it anyway.

Kassie liked it, him pressing up against her, holding her head gently with his hand while they kissed, but when people busted out of the restaurant laughing and shouting, she suddenly turned shy and put a stop to it.

It didn't take long to drive to the screening room. It was just an auditorium at Del Mar College, but they got there after the doors had opened, and a long line of stoked surfers had already gotten in. They had to sit in the back row.

The theater was packed. A giant beach ball bounced over the audience, people competing to make it bounce farther and higher than anyone else. The smell of reefer drifted over the auditorium.

When the lights went out the audience hooted—they yelled even louder as the movie started rolling.

The surf film clattered on the sixteen-millimeter projector set up at the back of the lecture hall. The soundtrack was at full volume. On the screen was Shaun Tomson, Wayne "Rabbit" Bartholomew, and Mark Richards dropping into incredible blue barrels, sliding right past the camera. The waves then rolled over the photographer, the footage capturing the surfers seen from inside the water, single fin stuck solid in the middle of the hollow, silvery barrel. Seeing this, the audience began hollering in a growing crescendo with the music. Tomson, in his sleeveless yellow zip vest and red shorts, dropped into a mesmerizing hollow tube ride in ultra-slow motion, approaching the camera as though he were going to crash right into it—but he coolly slid past so close that it seemed the viewer could reach out and touch him.

Seeing this, the auditorium crowd exploded with hoots and hollers, some even rising from their chairs in excitement.

Once the first rush of the film passed, Connor settled back down to what, as Maxim often said, "it was all about." He put his arm around Kassie, and she tucked into him, one hand on his thigh.

In the dark, she let it creep up higher, just to where he was starting to press stiff, then moving away again. Connor thrust forward toward her hand when it was at its closest—and yet she never caressed him in the way that he'd dreamed of uncountable times. They were, after all, in the middle of a crowded auditorium, watching a surfing movie.

By the time the last reel ended and the lights came on, both of them were so worked up that they quickly left, ignoring Maxim and some of the other surf-shop guys who had spotted them and waved.

"Let's go," Kassie said. "I don't want to talk to them."

Once outside, they headed straight for Connor's car, hand in hand, without speaking a word. The same thing seemed to be on both of their minds: to be alone with each other. Connor wasted no time getting out of the parking lot and heading back to Port Aransas.

FOURTEEN

VAGARIES HIGH ALOFT, temperature and pressure shifts, the piling up and sloughing away of gigantic air masses—tropospheric heating and cooling—those were the invisible and unknown things that began something special that wouldn't be noticed or reported in the newspapers or on TV for a few more days. But things were happening in the Gulf that would leave permanent memories.

Unaware of the developing weather, Connor and Kassie raced along the Island Road toward Port Aransas. Kassie sat nervously in the dark. In that moment, she just wished that they hadn't taken the Cutlass, even though it was nice.

"I want to sit closer to you," she said.

"Lift the center console," Connor said. "It folds back."

She did, then unbuckled her seat belt and scooted over. She kissed the side of his face and his neck, pulled on his earlobe with her lips, put her hand mid-thigh on his leg, moving up until she felt his hardness.

Connor's heart jumped. He was desperate to find the

beach access road he knew was somewhere up ahead. Kassie pressed her body and leg against his.

Warm. She felt warm, just like heaven.

Kassie had never perceived her body this way before—so taut inside, yet so comfortable—certainly not when she'd been a homecoming queen dating Andrew, the quarterback of the football team at Midland. She had never felt natural with him, like she did with Connor, who at the moment was the only thing in the world for her. She leaned in and spoke softly into his ear.

"I'm feeling emotions I don't know if I want to feel," she said, her hand rubbing him through his shorts.

"Sweet emotion?" Connor asked, grinning.

She turned more into him, so her breast pushed up against his arm, and softly kissed his neck and ear.

"I don't want to go home yet, Connor. I don't want you to take me home yet. I want to go down to the beach with you. Can we go down to the beach?"

Connor was having trouble controlling the speed of the Cutlass. He looked down and saw the speedometer showing ninety-five mph—and Kassie's hand firm on him through his shorts.

"Shit," he said, easing off the gas.

The road unreeled in front of him, the soft drone of the tires hummed, and Kassie's shadow form pressed against him. This was the real thing, better than any fantasy he'd ever had. He fumbled to put his right arm around her in the dark. He was so hard that it was almost cracking against his surf baggies, and Kassie knew it. Her hand ran over his shorts, clasped him one way, then another; it was warm, thick, and filled her grip. Inside, she felt like she was melting, like this car needed to stop at once—right now, on the shoulder. Every fiber of her being was wanting him inside her.

At last, Connor saw the little green sign he was looking for growing bright in the headlights:

Beach Access Road No. 2

"You're so hard," Kassie said. "I think you need to be out of those Birdwells."

Kassie inhaled the scent of coconut suntan oil behind Connor's ear. Without restraint, she leaned in and softly nuzzled it. She moved her hand over his lap, Connor raised his hips in response. She worked the tip out, her fingers pulling on hot flesh.

"Oh, man, Kassie," he muttered.

"Don't come yet," she commanded.

"No," he said, dumbfounded.

Connor pulled off the highway and onto the beach access road.

"I think you need to do something," she whispered. "I've thought about it so many times, and now you're going to do it."

Connor parked close to the water, turned off the lights. He put the electric windows down and they heard the white noise from the surf, the thump of small waves breaking.

He didn't talk, but kissed Kassie instead.

She felt him, firm and hot, and a small part of her was terrified. The rest of her was in control.

"Your clothes," she said, pulling at the hem of his shorts. "They're bothering me."

"What the hell am I thinking?" he said. He undid the heavy string that tied his shorts to his body, and Kassie tried to help get them off. They stubbornly resisted and Connor banged his knees against the steering wheel trying to get them off.

"Ow!" he said.

Kassie laughed.

"Don't you dare hurt it," she said, covering his lap with her hand to protect it.

Connor managed to get the Birdwells off one leg, then the other. They embraced awkwardly in the car. Kassie wanted it—wanted him—right now. Maybe it was the alcohol, maybe it wasn't. It didn't matter. She found herself pulled like a magnet to Connor's heat. His hands roamed through her hair: her head went down, fingers of her left hand splayed on his chest, clutching his pec.

But that wasn't what he was paying attention to.

It was like she had fantasized, but saltier, firmer, hotter. After a moment, she lifted her head.

"Oh, my God," she whispered.

Then she plunged down again. She'd only read about it clandestinely in a *Penthouse* magazine that her friend Alex had pilfered from her dad. The oral sex letter to the editor, supposedly written by a woman, had rocked her imagination.

But this was way more exciting.

Connor was nearly delirious. This had never happened to him before. All he'd ever felt before was his hand; this was different, a soft and firm envelopment he'd never known.

"Oh, my God," he said, as tension built. Gently, he clutched both sides of her head.

She lifted up and looked at him. Her breath smelled faintly of tequila from the margaritas they'd had—clean like her own mouth and lips—but also earthy. She was out of breath, and her eyes were wide.

"I've never done this," she said.

"I haven't, either."

Then it was all arms and legs, elbows banging faces and fingers poking awkwardly. They laughed at each other's clumsiness as they shed their clothes. Connor shoved the seats back as far as they would go, leaned them back until both he and Kassie had room. She was on her back, under him, on the velour black upholstery of his dad's Cutlass Supreme. Connor reached up and turned on the radio, which began playing Aerosmith's "Dream On."

"It's a sign," Kassie said.

They both felt something new—naked flesh on each other—and nothing in their lives had ever even come close to feeling so full and complete as this moment did. Kassie held onto Connor's head, staring into his eyes.

"Now," she said. "Do it."

Connor's heart wasn't racing. This was just the right thing to do.

He pressed, but missed.

He pressed again—missed once more.

There was a moment of levity when she giggled, which for Connor threatened the heat of the moment, but Kassie took care of that, reaching down, showing him the way.

"There," she said.

He felt her slick.

"Slow," she said.

And that is how it was: slow, with both of their eyes getting bigger. It was more work than he had expected, but the power coming from Kassie made him grow stronger until suddenly he was inside.

Her hips thrust gently up against his, and they were locked together, neither one ever having done this before.

"Connor?" Kassie said.

"What?" he asked.

"Do it," she commanded. "Do it like you mean it."

Connor did.

This isn't going to last long, he thought. The feelings

coursing through him at that moment would lead to only one result. The surf was building outside, like the pressure building in Connor's body; Kassie's face was starting to look like dark ecstasy. She moaned and grabbed his hips, pulling him into her. The surf outside was somehow thudding in the distance, like it was suddenly eight feet high and rising, but out of sync with their movements, too fast. Kassie heard it, started to look uncertain. It got louder and choppier, a definite rhythmic thudding—and then the shocking realization hit them both as a Coast Guard helicopter roared over the beach, swinging its search light back and forth.

A white flash illuminated the inside of the car.

Connor saw Kassie's face, bright white in the blaze, a look of shock on it, their bodies embracing, outlined in expressionistic black and white.

Then the light was gone, the chopper kept going, hauling ass, flying straight south as it scanned the water and beach with its bright eye.

"No," Kassie blurted.

Her legs squeezed against Connor.

"Connor ... no."

His heart was pounding in his chest, but her command came not a moment too soon. Even one more thrust would have done it. He ceased his movement, withdrew, lifted himself up so he wasn't touching her.

She said stop. So he stopped.

The thudding of the helicopter was fading, but the shock it left behind was growing.

"Are you OK?" he asked.

"Yes."

Unbelievable. Freaking Coast Guard, thought Connor.

He watched through the passenger-side window as the helicopter disappeared in the distance. Soon, all he saw was the darting search light and its tail beacon firing at intervals. Kassie's eyes were closed, and her hands folded across her breasts. Her face was screwed up like she was in pain.

"Are you OK?" he asked again.

"I'm sorry," she said.

Then, to Connor's surprise, she wept.

FIFTEEN

CONNOR WAS HAVING a hard time accepting Kassie's words about what had just happened. It had been uncontrollable magnetism—then she had switched it off instantly. She caused them to separate, yet the lust for him was still shining on her face when they got back to her condo, when she shut the door after getting out of the Cutlass. She had looked in at him, smiling, lingering.

"That was so much fun. Thank you, baby."

Then she dashed up the steps. When she got to her floor she stopped and leaned over the railing.

"Connor," she called out.

Connor poked his head out the driver's-side window and looked up at her.

"I've got to go fishing with my parents tomorrow morning," she said. "See you after?"

"To hell with fishing," he shouted. "Let's go surfing again!"

Kassie giggled.

"Shush. Not so loud, silly! You'll wake my parents up. I'll call you, OK?"

"OK."

Then she disappeared into her condo.

Connor felt deflated as he started the Cutlass.

"I'm still a freaking virgin," he muttered as he backed out, then immediately felt like an ass.

It wasn't about something so stupid as that, he thought.

While he drove the two minutes back home, he felt everything at once. Elation and frustration, victory and defeat. They'd consummated all the flirting and teasing, the intense desires he'd been feeling since Kassie had arrived two weeks ago—she'd wanted him inside—but just as it became true and honest ... the helicopter.

"Damn Coast Guard!" Connor yelled, thumping his steering wheel as he pulled into Gulf Beach Cottages.

He squarely blamed the chopper's sweep down the beach, which likely had been a planned practice run for spotting drowning victims in the surf. In frustration, he cranked up the car's stereo, listened to Moxy's "Still I Wonder," and felt like a loser at the conclusion of the greatest moment of his life.

Kassie closed the condo door, relieved that her dad wasn't sitting up waiting for her. He'd be able to tell she was a hot mess. Quickly, quietly, she went to her bedroom, shut the door, and locked it. Without taking off her clothes, she got in bed, still feeling the deep flush from when Connor had been inside her. She rolled over, putting her hands between her thighs. It was still hot down there.

She rolled over again and stared at the ceiling.

What the hell had she done? What if she got pregnant? She knew she was getting close to her period. What if some sperm had gotten inside of her? How could she explain that to her parents? She should have kept doing it with her mouth. It's what she'd been fantasizing about, anyway. She blamed what had happened on the heat of the moment.

"Well," she whispered, "isn't Connor exactly what I want? So what if I get pregnant? I can still go to school. He'll be a stay-at-home dad."

The thought of Connor trying to change a baby's diaper made her laugh.

But the whole thing wasn't very funny. There were so many guys after her that she could have her pick.

She thought: *If dudes can get laid whenever they want, why can't I?*

But when she thought about other guys, somehow Connor would show up in the picture.

She'd wanted it. She'd wanted *him*.

Kassie could imagine her mom, angry, saying something she'd never ever say: "So you risked it all and were going to just let him come inside you, until suddenly some random helicopter searchlight made you think God was watching? You're an idiot!"

There was no way her mom would let her take the pill, she thought, even if she did shift her position on premarital sex. And condoms—Kassie could imagine her mom's eyes bugging out of her head at the suggestion. It had felt so good, knowing it was him about to come inside her. She lusted after it, wanted to hear him call her name when he did, then hold him tight with her legs around his body. She felt guilty for having had sex but at the same time wished she hadn't made him stop. What she wanted was him lying with her in this bed, right now, cuddled up until their breathing calmed and they would just lay there, falling into dream together. Then they could let the light of that helicopter shine on them for God and everyone else to see. It was, after all, the truth.

SIXTEEN

THE SEED of the storm germinated when hot air from Mexico swept northward over the warm waters of the Gulf for hundreds of miles, until it collided with cooler air coming south from high over southeastern Florida. Cool, descending high-pressure air crashed into the moisture-laden Mexican tropical wave and spurred a tropical depression that formed above the Yucatan Peninsula.

The meteorologists named it Debra, and it caused a stir at the surf shop when Stamford came in and announced its presence.

"It'll be on the news tonight, for sure," he said. "Got a call putting me on evac alert. All the other boats, too. Three rigs got crews on 'em that might need to get pulled."

They went over to a large, plasticized map of the Gulf, and Stamford stabbed his finger just above Yucatan.

"Debra's here, moving west. Well, northwest."

"Wind?" Maxim asked.

"Sustained forty-two, heading higher."

Maxim perked up.

"Shit, that's looking good," he said. "If she can just keep going north and get stronger she'll give us some nice, lined-up waves for once. Wind might suck, though."

"Actually, I read there's a weak cold front coming down," Sandi said. "Supposed to get here in three days."

"Holy shit," Maxim whispered. "An offshore wind, a tropical storm—maybe even a hurricane?"

"Dunno," Stamford said. "It's good juju, though. Very good juju."

The condo phone rang. Kassie's mom picked up.

"Hi, it's Connor," the voice on the line said. "Is Kassie there?"

"She went down to the beach."

"She did?"

Connor fumbled through saying goodbye. Kassie had told him she'd call, and he'd been feeling good about getting to see her, but now she was at the beach and hadn't called him. An image of Kassie surrounded by guys came to mind. It made him mad.

Why do I feel like this? he asked himself. *This is bullshit. She just wanted to go down to the beach. What's the big deal?*

He thought of her dancing with Maxim, or how she enjoyed the attention from him at Boxcar Billy's. Maybe she was with some guys from San Antonio, or Corpus, from anywhere and everywhere—

Connor grabbed his car keys and went out of his room. His dad was sitting on the couch, reading, but looked up over his glasses.

"Hey, how was your date last night with that girl you met from Midland? What was her name again?"

"Kassie. It was great. The surf movie was especially great."

"I noticed you came home pretty late."

"Yes."

Connor didn't want to chit-chat right now. He wanted to find Kassie.

"So, did you get laid?"

"Aw, come on, Dad. Don't embarrass me," Connor said. "You know I don't like to talk about stuff like that."

"Just making sure you're not gonna get all excited and leave me here in Port Aransas while you go chasing tail halfway across the States."

"Oh, my God," Connor said, rolling his eyes and heading out. "OK. See ya."

Connor closed the door and shuddered. He had to find Kassie. He had a terrible feeling she might be hanging out with one of his other friends. Or maybe Maxim was all over her. That would be the end of it right there. He couldn't put up with anything like that. Not after what had happened last night with her. Not after what had happened with his mom and dad.

Before his mom left Texas, she'd lied to him over the phone.

"It's not you, Connor," she'd told him. "I just can't be with your dad anymore. I want to go back to school, but he says I need to stay home and be focused on the family. There are other problems, but I can't burden you with those. I'll be close, right here in Texas. Don't worry."

But she didn't stay close. It was almost two months after she left that a letter arrived, telling him that she'd been accepted into a master's degree program in Colorado Springs.

"I'll fly you up every couple of months," she had written, but she never flew him up. Nor did she write frequently. He was lucky to hear from her every few months. At first he got letters, then postcards, then nothing.

Connor got in his truck and headed for the beach. He had to know what Kassie was doing—and who she was doing it with. He knew that it was wrong, but he couldn't help himself. Just last night they were as close as human beings could get, but now she'd gone to the beach without telling him.

"Jeez," he muttered, knowing his jealousy was completely out of control. "Maybe I've lost my ever-lovin' mind. I mean, can a girl go to the damn beach without being spied on?"

SEVENTEEN

KASSIE WAS DOZING when she heard a car pull up nearby, then a door open and close. She turned her head and saw Connor walking toward her. Immediately, her heart jumped with excitement—but when she looked at him, she wasn't sure what his face was showing. Was he angry?

"Hi," he said. "I was just driving down the beach and thought I saw you. And ... well, I did see you."

He was wearing red Birdwells, a T-shirt, and a Denver Broncos cap.

"I was just thinking about you," Kassie said.

That was no lie. She'd been thinking all night and all morning about Connor. No matter how she contemplated things, she kept coming back to love versus ambition, passion versus goals. There were things she'd wanted since she was a kid; she'd watched her dad go to work at NASA every day and come home with incredible stories. There were those times when Buzz Aldrin had come by to work with her dad on trans-lunar and trans-Earth injection burns. She had been told to not bother them, but Buzz had been nice to her.

"You going to be an astronaut when you grow up?" he'd asked, when he spied her peeking around the corner. "Best stop lurking and come learn some physics."

She came out in the open, thrilled by the invitation, but her dad had shooed her away.

"I've been thinking about you, too," Connor said, bringing her back to the present.

"Good thoughts?"

"Always."

Kassie wanted to tell him that she wished she hadn't told him to stop the other night. She wished she'd just pulled him into her, over and over, until ...

"Connor, about last night. I –"

"It's all right," he interrupted. "I lost control, and you ... you just do things to me. You do them, and I lose control. Maybe I shouldn't have."

"I'm glad you did," she said.

Connor looked at her eyes. She was looking right into his.

"Sit down with me," Kassie said, patting the sand next to her towel. "I want to talk."

Oh, great, Connor thought. *Here it comes. Dear John in person.*

Connor sat, looking at her beauty. First down to her feet, then up to her face. But he was glum, expecting the worst.

"So I don't need to apologize?" he asked.

"For last night? Why would you apologize? I wanted you as bad as you wanted me."

Connor stared at the small waves lapping the shore, suspicious of the past tense she was using to describe her desire. A stray gull swooped around looking for tidbits on the sand. Maybe she'd decided it was not good for her future to have the kinds of feelings they had for each other.

"*Wanted?*" he asked, accenting the past tense she'd used.

"Oh," Kassie said, reaching out and putting her hand on his thigh. "*Want.* I *want* you as badly as you want me. I was just going to tell you that I wish I hadn't asked you to stop."

Connor was surprised, relief flashing through his whole body.

"Oh, my God," he said as he laid down on the sand beside her.

He laughed, and Kassie let go of his thigh and propped herself up on her elbows.

"Hey, what's so funny?" she asked.

"Well," he answered, "I'm just a moron. I thought ... actually, never mind what I thought."

Kassie looked out at the water. What she had to say next was not going to be easy.

"Listen, Connor," she said, almost embarrassed. "In January, I'm going off to California. You know I got a scholarship offer to UC San Diego for aerospace engineering. The director of the program there is named Dr. Libby. He runs the show, sort of like Franklin's dad runs the show at the Marine Science Institute here in Port A. Dr. Libby does heat-shield research. Even though I'm totally in ... I mean ... well, I just have to go."

Even though I'm totally in love with you, Connor thought, filling in the words she hadn't said but had wanted to. He felt certain of it. He smiled big as he reached out and took her hand in his.

"Yes, you do have to go to San Diego, Kassie. I mean you are the most incredible girl I've ever met. Here I am in Port Aransas doing jack all. I haven't figured it out yet. I'm tired of being in school. I just need a break. I need to quiet my mind. I wanted to wait until next year to decide about college. But then here you come—a big, loud ruckus, completely blowing my mind—the best kind of ruckus ever."

Connor let his gaze wander out to the water, then looked up toward the Gulf Coast sun. Its burn, so bright and painful as it mercilessly baked the Texas coast, was being blunted by a low, thin layer of clouds. A light wind blew. Something was brewing.

Right in front of them, maybe twenty yards out in the relatively flat Gulf, a bottlenose dolphin's fin broke the surface, then two more.

"That," he said, pointing. "See? That's my future right there. I know it is. Just not right now, not right here."

Seeing the small pod of bottlenose dolphins made Kassie smile.

"You know, Connor, there's not just a marine science institute here at Port A. There's also one in San Diego."

She looked at him, and he knew she'd just given him an invitation.

"I shouldn't say this," Kassie said. "I'm scared to say this, but I'm going to say it anyway. It's you, Connor. Now. Last night, tomorrow, everything I'm thinking about has you in it—here, next semester at San Diego. You know what that means? I think I'm ... "

She faltered, grabbed some sand in her hand and looked at it.

"You think you're ... what?" Connor asked, trying to get her to say what he knew.

"I proved to you last night what I think I am."

Connor almost said, "You mean ... a bad girl?"

But he caught himself. It was the wrong moment for a joke. Besides, he surely was just as "bad" as she was, and neither one of them was like Stamford; they had simply done the natural thing.

Suddenly, a horn blared, and a man hooted loudly, catcalling at Kassie.

"Whoo, baby!" he shouted. "Oh, yeah!"

It was Stamford.

His truck turned abruptly toward them, coming up too fast—and too close—but he whipped away at the last second. Kassie jumped up, angry.

"What the hell, man?" she yelled.

"What the hell, indeed," Stamford said, shutting down his truck and getting out. Then, in a sarcastic voice, he added: "So, how are the two lovebirds?"

Connor was about to tell Stamford to fuck off, but Stamford held his hand out.

"Peace, man. Peace. You know I'm always just messing around, always joking. Listen, I just thought you'd want to know there's a full-on tropical storm out in the Gulf right now. Seems to be cruising straight north. It might even turn into a hurricane. Best chance for good waves we've had all summer. I mean, Connor's been teaching you to surf—right, Kassie?"

"Right," she said, arms akimbo. She wanted to kick him in the balls.

"Anyhoo," Stamford said with a drawl, "all this crap you see right now is about to transform into long lines of bad-ass, offshore tickled wedges. You just wait. It's supposed to hit this Saturday."

Connor reached out and touched Kassie's elbow. When she looked at him, she saw Connor was smirking.

"So, hey, maybe on Saturday we can show Stamford all the progress you've made. It might get a little big, though, for a beginner."

Kassie caught the hint and played along.

"Oh, man," she said. "I mean, how big do you think?"

"Four to six feet at the third bar," Stamford said. "Six to eight further out. Maybe even ten."

"Oh, my God," Kassie said.

"I'll be putting on a good show, so have your camera ready," Stamford said.

Then, pointing at Connor, he added: "Better than that guy, anyway. Hell, Kassie, if it's too big, you can hang out on the beach or on the pier with Sandi. She surfs sometimes, but sometimes she just waxes Maxim's board."

Stamford slapped his knee and busted out laughing at his own joke.

"Get it?" Stamford said. "She waxes his board!"

"Always the charmer," Connor replied.

"Hey, one other thing," Stamford said. "My deckhand gave notice. I figure you might like earning sixteen-fifty an hour to start. Pelican's will be closing soon, you need a job, and I need a deckhand. Perfect team, just like always, brother."

Connor had been wondering what he'd be doing once Pelican's Wharf closed for the summer.

"Sixteen-fifty?" Connor asked, surprised. That was more per hour than he earned at Pelican's, by far.

"Yup," Stamford said. "And that's just to start. My deckhand was up to nineteen an hour, but he wanted to go apprentice being a captain on another boat."

"Cool," Connor said, warming to the idea of making some decent loot. "Minimum wage is what, two-fifty?"

"Two sixty-five," Stamford said. "Now if you two lovebirds will excuse me, I've got a date with a real hottie from Dallas. It's gonna be a long night, my friends. A long night."

Stamford got in his truck, powered up, and cranked AC/DC, his perennial favorite, started pounding the side of his truck door and shouting the lyrics to "Problem Child" completely out of key.

He drove off, trying to spray them with sand, but missed and fishtailed down the beach.

"See ya, Stamford" Kassie said as she flipped him off.

Being brave, she looked squarely at Connor.

"So, crew boat work?" she asked.

Connor couldn't handle her gaze, so he stared out at the Gulf. He watched a flock of seagulls fly past. After a moment, he turned back to her, his eyes looking everywhere but at hers, a lump in his throat.

"Yeah, well, either that or I was thinking about maybe checking the surf on the West Coast," he said. "I hear the Pacific's not too cold down south. You know, like Black's or Windansea?"

Kassie reached over and took Connor's hand.

"Look," she said.

He looked.

The soft wind was moving a few strands of her hair, and he felt suddenly whole, not standing taller, not shorter; now they were just alone and comfortable and could make any decision they wanted.

"I'm not lying about it," she said. "I have strong feelings about you and about going to school, too. Maybe I'm confused. I don't know what to do about it yet. But I have to take this scholarship, Connor. No woman in my family has ever gone to college. I'm the first one. My parents—well, they need me to do this, especially my mom, even though she doesn't say so. Do you understand?"

Connor felt the pang of sorrow he felt when his mom had written to him to say she had been accepted to a master's program. He looked away from Kassie. His mom hadn't asked him to come to Colorado, and he wouldn't have gone anyway because he was angry at her—and back then he was still in high school. He had graduated now, and he wasn't angry anymore, but he still missed her.

He waited to see if Kassie would ask him to come with her, but she didn't.

"I don't know how to explain anymore," she said, still holding his hand and looking at him. "But you get why I have to go, don't you?"

"Yeah," he said after a moment. "Yeah, I get it."

EIGHTEEN

TROPICAL STORM DEBRA'S winds increased steadily as it moved northwest before shifting course to due north, but it never made hurricane status on its march toward Beaumont and Lake Charles. The maximum measured winds peaked at sixty, but that didn't matter; the storm didn't have to become a full-blown hurricane to deliver the goods to surfers waiting impatiently in Port Aransas. The combo of offshore winds and widely spaced waves was ideal.

The first signs were a deep-green calming water. The weak cold front approaching from the north caused an incredibly powerful side-shore wind that dampened everyone's hopes, but then it just stopped. The stillness was eerie, the cross chop vanished. That Friday evening, smallish waves were developing with the classic wedge-shaped form. The waves spread further apart, first twenty to thirty yards, then fifty to sixty, getting bigger by the moment.

Maxim was at the pier, looking out to sea.

Far out beyond the seven-mile visible horizon of the Gulf,

he could see the tops of cumulonimbus storm clouds. They were the smaller thunderstorms gathering around Debra's heart. Lightning flashes lit up the darkening eastern sky. He'd left the shop early because Sandi was going to close up. Maxim wanted those storms to bring good waves. He wished for it, willed it, all his thought was bent on it.

A small three-footer rolled in under the pier, broke, and was big enough to make the wood structure lurch a little and creak. He loved the sound of waves smashing on the pilings.

Maxim pulled half a joint from his pack of Marlboro cigarettes. He lit it and toked until it was gone, getting seriously high. It was the best Oaxacan to be found.

He thought about the winds blowing far out on the vast stretches of the Gulf, building up a swell that would combine and pile up to become ever larger and larger, originating from just outside Debra's eye, where the winds would be at their absolute strongest. From there they would move through the deep water, built up by the circulating winds all along their route. Soon enough, the waves would leave behind the wind but keep on coming. They would arrive here, just underneath where he was standing. Here at Port Aransas, and the winds would be slightly offshore, blowing in the opposite direction the waves were moving. It was a perfect combination of weather elements that almost never coincided. The waves would still have their potency when they arrived, while the pier, now barely moved by the three-foot surf, would by tomorrow afternoon start to shudder at the passing of each successively larger set of waves.

This will be the best surf we've had in years, Maxim thought.

Pleasantly stoned, he turned and strolled back past the fishermen toward the beach, paused for a moment to watch one yanking up a three-foot sand shark. It freaked coming out of the water, thrashing so madly that its small teeth cut through the line the guy had on his rig. It plunged back into the water. The man who'd lost it started shouting and cursing in Spanish.

The shark darted away in the green.

NINETEEN

THE SUN WAS JUST COMING over the eastern horizon when Connor went to pick Kassie up. He left Gulf Beach Cottages straight for the Sea Isle condos. Exiting the driveway, he couldn't tell how good the waves were because of the sunrise glare. He arrived quickly at Kassie's condo and went up the stairs to her unit. She let him in before he knocked, hugged him briefly, then told him to keep his voice low. She had just made a pot of coffee, and the aroma filled the air. After pouring them each a cup, she handed him a pack of chocolate-covered mini-doughnuts.

Connor chuckled.

"How did you know I liked chocolate doughnuts?" he asked.

"I saw the wrappers on the floorboard of your truck," she said.

Connor dug into them. He thought they were great, even though they coated his teeth with waxy residue. It was an excellent energy rush before an early morning surf.

"You brought the Weber Winger, didn't you?" Kassie

asked. "It'll be squirrely as hell if the waves are as big as Stamford said, but it's crazy responsive."

"Sure," Connor said. "If you want, we can trade out sometimes. I brought my Lightning Bolt."

"A real one?"

"Signed by Terry Martin himself."

"Cool!"

They quickly finished their coffee so they could head to the beach. Both of them were amped about the surf and wanted to know how big the waves were.

When Connor's truck rounded the bend on Sandcastle Drive, they freaked at what they saw.

"Oh, man!" Kassie yelled. "Look at that. Waves clear out to the horizon!"

"Look at those corduroy lines!" Connor said.

The waves were coming in beautiful, distinct sets.

"I cannot believe this," Kassie murmured.

"Maybe we should have done a pre-dawn patrol," Connor said. "Who knows how many good waves we've missed?"

"Hurry up!" Kassie replied. "Get us to the pier!"

Connor sped north, well above the fifteen-mile-an-hour speed limit. Kassie's mind was blown as much as Connor's. She knew how crappy Gulf Coast waves were most of the time, having spent some summers at Clear Lake. Her mom had driven them down to Galveston, where Kassie had surfed as much as possible.

They pulled up near the pier and saw that the waves were breaking consistently beyond the third bar. The morning sun, still low in the sky, backlit the waves and caused a line of bright-green luminescence to flash along the wall as it went vertical. The gentle offshore breeze feathered the waves and blew a rain of saltwater droplets over each one.

"Jeez," Connor said, totally amping. He jumped out of the truck.

Kassie got out and hooted.

"Wow!" she said, watching as a big set wave pitched out and forward, making a hollow section peel both left and right.

Connor just stared, jaw open, as he watched a surfer race down a perfectly formed right that kept going vertical all the way down the line. The surfer was compressed by g-forces so powerful that he crouched perpendicular to the vertical wave face. He pumped the board lightly up and down, dropped into a backside crouch, then raced into a section that barreled him for twenty yards. Then the wave collapsed into whitewater. A black dot of a head surfaced, followed by an arm pumping a fist over and over as the surfboard gently drifted nearby.

"We've got to get out there, right now!" Connor said.

Kassie threw him a piece of Mr. Zog's, and they both started furiously rubbing the wax over their boards, which smelled of fake coconut and paraffin. As they worked, other cars and trucks with surfboards pulled up, hoots and hollers, no one paying any attention to Kassie for once.

"It shouldn't take too long to paddle out if we stick close to the pier," Kassie said as she saw the other surfers being pulled out in the channel flow right next to the pilings.

"Or we could jump off the end," Connor said.

Kassie looked at him mischievously.

"Let's do it," she said.

TWENTY

STAMFORD SAW the perfect wedge and paddled full speed. As the wall of water started sucking him upward, he whipped around and stroked once, twice, then felt the wave lift him. He glanced right and left, then went right. It was a view he had never seen outside the pages of a surf magazine: The glassy dark green wave tapered off for at least fifty or sixty yards, head high when he dropped in, and the lip sprayed water back over the wave as it pitched.

Other surfers hooted as he carved a hard bottom turn, spraying a fan of water high in the air. He drove down the line, climbing and dropping, then the arc of the wave pitched over, thin, hollow, translucent. It wrapped him inside. He looked out from the eye of the barrel. His board bouncing on the foam ball, he hooted wildly, until a second later the wave collapsed on him. He was tossed and yanked underwater like a rag doll.

After the tumbling stopped, he popped up, used the leash to pull his board back to him, blew the saltwater out of his nose, spit it out of his mouth, and started stroking back out toward the lineup.

He glanced up and saw two figures jump from the end of the pier—one of them a chick.

Stamford arrived back at the lineup and sat upright on his board.

"Dude," said Franklin, "You got so tubed!"

Stamford was smiling from ear to ear.

"Better than most sex, my friend," he said, grinning.

"Let's go to the fourth bar," Kassie yelled, pointing farther out.

They were just beyond where the waves were breaking on the third bar, which was head-high and perfect, with occasional tubes. But it was somewhat crowded, even for the Gulf Coast. Guys were cutting each other off already, and though the waves out at the fourth bar were a little more infrequent, they were definitely bigger—and empty. No one was out there.

Connor felt a small pang of fear course through him at Kassie's suggestion.

If it had been anyone else, he might've said no, but he didn't want to let on that he was scared about something she was asking to do. Instead, they both stroked farther out, toward the fourth bar, where the waves were breaking at least another fifty or sixty yards beyond the pier's T-head. Every time Connor got a little freaked by the size of the waves that went past, he just looked over at Kassie, slightly ahead of him, who looked so incredible and powerful and confident as she paddled through the water. She didn't seem to have the slightest inhibition or fear—and that inspired him.

When they got to the lineup, they were alone.

The overhead waves came in sets of six to ten, some not quite tall enough to break. Out here, any wave smaller than eight feet wasn't going to break. Connor felt the water's depth and power in his bones. He could imagined being far out to sea in swell this size; no sand ever under your feet, no bottom, just an endless depth filled with carnivorous beasts.

Kassie sat on the Winger a few feet away, squinting at the sun reflecting off the water. She kept shaking her head.

"I didn't think the Gulf had it in her," she said to Connor. "This is as good as Cali. It's probably better than Waikiki."

In that moment, a good set hove into view, looking like it would break twenty yards to the right of them. Kassie snapped to paddling toward where the wave was going to peak.

"Damn!" shouted Connor. "You're crazy, girl!"

Kassie turned her head and grinned.

"Come on!" she shouted. "We need to catch some of these while we've got 'em to ourselves."

Connor looked toward the pier, the T-head probably a good seventy yards further in. He saw a few other surfers starting to point toward them. Nobody was coming out yet, though. They wanted to see what would happen.

Kassie was paddling fast. At the base of the thick, green wall, she spun her board about and stroked hard as the wave wedged up under her; a beam of light blitzed through the top of the emerald lip, spray feathering as it peaked. She snapped to her feet as the top of the wave started to crash down. It seemed twice her height, but she rocketed downward with masterly balance. At the bottom she banged an incredible turn—spray flying wildly. Connor heard other surfers hooting and shouting approval. Kassie blasted down the line and climbed up, cut back hard at the top, then went straight back down. Crystal droplets of water hung glittering in the air. As she climbed and dropped, the wave started to section ahead of her. She aimed straight toward the pinnacle of two sections of whitewater which were coming together and pulled an off-the-lip so vertical that the board almost launched out of the wave. Instantly, she snapped around to point downward again, her hair fanning in an arc.

She landed it solid and screeched, chased by a wall of whitewater.

Connor yelled.

Kassie fought for stability, adrenaline roiling inside her as hard as the whitewater pushing her from behind. She swept past Connor, then kicked out twenty yards further on as the wave started to reform in deeper water between the sandbars.

Kassie was stoked raw as she paddled back out. Connor just stared at her as she pulled up right next to him, bumping his board with hers as she sat up.

"Whoo!" she said. "Damn, that felt *good!*"

Then she did something Connor loved: She pulled him into her and kissed him. She tasted like the sea.

"Can you believe this?" she asked, sweeping her arm north to south over the long length of the beach break.

Connor heard the hoots and hollers further in. There was no question what would happen next. Some of the surfers at the third bar were going to come out to the fourth. Kassie looked around, seeing the distant figures stroking to come join them.

"'Damn," she said. "That didn't last long."

After a couple more smaller sets came through—ones with waves not big enough to break on the fourth bar—Connor heard Stamford's unmistakable voice: "God *damn. God damn!* can you believe that shit, y'all? That was Kassie Hernandez!"

Connor looked over his shoulder. Stamford was just getting out to the lineup, his eyes popping.

Maxim, next to Stamford, paddled up to Connor and playfully punched his arm.

"Dude," he said, smiling really big and nodding toward Kassie. "Way to go, brother."

Then Maxim paddled over to Kassie and held up his hand for a high-five.

"You have seriously got it going on, girl! That was the best ride I've seen in a long time."

"Aww," Kassie said. "I just borrowed some of that wave's juice."

Connor felt he needed to show what he could do. He saw a hefty incoming prospect starting to wall up, and as a bunch of dudes were beginning to circle around Kassie, he lay down on his board and stroked toward the approaching wave.

He could tell the wave was going to peak about fifteen yards to the right of where he was, so he paddled as hard as he could to get into position. It jacked up much higher than he expected—a wall so steep that it threatened to break on top of him before he could drop in.

Other surfers saw him and began hooting and hollering; Connor spun, stroked twice, then snapped up.

The drop was so fast that the board almost fell out from under him, but the slight offshore breeze held the lip back just long enough for him to make it to the bottom and turn right. He saw the long wall wedging up perfectly as far as he could see, dots of surfers in the water watching him. Instinctively, he crouched as the top of the wave pitched over in a flattened oval.

Connor was in the eye of the barrel.

Time slowed. The tube was solid, with a rush of air and water and the roar of the foam ball. His board bounced wildly. Just in that prime moment of the wave lip arcing over, seeing out the formed eye, Stamford loomed in Connor's line of sight. His friend's sudden appearance was a jolt of negative energy, ruining the most electric moment Connor had ever felt while surfing. His eye-shaped crystal world focused on Stamford's shocked face, slack-jawed and ten feet in front, one arm reaching forward, one arm trailing behind, neither moving. Connor's surfboard would impale him, run over him just like Stamford had run over Connor two years back.

In a blur, Connor bailed into the wave face. It yanked him up and over the falls. He triumphantly screeched a stream of bubbles underwater, then spewed a mouthful of saltwater when he broke the surface. He was ecstatic.

Kassie was hooting at him, sitting on her board just a few yards away.

"That was *rad!*" she shouted, her eyes popping. "If you hadn't had to bail because of Stamford, you'd still be in the barrel. Freaking *crazy!*"

Connor pulled himself up on his board, adrenaline coursing through his whole body. All he could think about was doing it again. A moment later he noticed Stamford, who was gazing over at him with a strange look on his face.

"I'm sorry, dude," his friend said.

Here, on the Texas Coast, a tube ride was so rare that to ruin another surfer's barrel was an unforgivable sin.

Connor smiled.

"No sweat, dude," he said. "We'll have more like that before the day is done!"

They kept surfing all morning. As the waves started to get smaller, they kept at it anyway, moving to the third bar, then finally to the second bar. They knew that today they had to extract everything they could out of the Gulf. Tomorrow, it would be flat.

Slowly, the guys who Kassie ignored gave up their vain hopes and started vying for waves among each other, yelling and dropping in on each other, but they still allowed her to catch whatever she wanted.

Maxim was sticking close, talking, complimenting, advising.

Kassie would listen to him talk and smile, but when a wave she wanted approached, she'd hold up her finger at him, lay down on her board, and paddle into takeoff position.

Every time she paddled off, Maxim blatantly stared at her ass.

"Damn," he said at one point, after Kassie paddled into a position twenty yards away scouting for incoming waves. He looked over at Connor, nonchalantly said: "Don't know if I can keep my distance, brother."

Connor smiled at Maxim.

"Nobody can," he said. "So that won't set you apart."

Maxim looked surprised by Connor's bit of wisdom. Then he shrugged, lay down on his board, and paddled over to where Kassie sat scrutinizing the Gulf.

Connor stayed where he was.

TWENTY-ONE

LUST.

It was no news to Kassie. It happened to her everywhere she surfed, unless she managed to go out all by herself. She had discovered, though, as irritating as these guys were, that she could exploit her looks to get more waves. Nobody called, "My wave, my wave!" when she turned to paddle for a big one. No one dropped in on her. All of them held back and yelled for her to go for it. They'd watch her carve and shred mercilessly.

Connor wasn't sure what part of the show they enjoyed most. Some of them seemed to be a little annoyed at how good she was, but nobody wanted to ruin a chance they might have with her later on the beach, when the surfing was done. So she took all those reluctantly hopeful gifts and paddled tirelessly into one wave, then another. Every time one of the surfers paddled close to her and tried to talk, she just watched the waves, maybe nodding her head as she threw out a few smiles to keep hope alive. No one was keeping count, but it seemed to Connor that she caught more good waves—and had more amazing rides—than anyone else. He watched the cream of the local surfers riding their absolute best, being their coolest selves possible, trying to impress her.

Connor still felt confident, but the writing was on the wall. Kassie was so hot, so talented, that she'd be able to pick any guy she wanted. He knew he wasn't as cool or good-looking as some of the surfers who now swirled around Kassie wherever she was paddling.

And yet she had told him how she felt. It was a question of trust. And in the moment, he was able to smile as he looked at all the wannabe lovers making convo with a girl who just wanted to catch some good waves and have a good time surfing.

About one in the afternoon, the waves started to falter on the second bar. Kassie paddled over to Connor, an exhausted smile on her face, while behind her all the guys were watching her. She sat up on her board.

"Well," she said. "I guess we can't expect the waves to get bigger again."

"Nope."

"You tired?"

"My arms feel like spaghetti noodles."

"Then let's go in," she said.

Connor followed her as the two-foot whitewater walls at the second bar pushed them toward shore, strong enough to keep them going all the way in until the bottoms of their boards dug into the sandy bottom just offshore.

They got up, rinsed the sand off the boards, and returned to Connor's truck.

The beach was littered with surfboards. Men and women gathered in small groups, smoking weed and drinking beer. Sandi had a small fire going in a pit.

Connor and Kassie put their boards in the his truck bed,

put towels around their shoulders, and stood at the front, leaning against the grill and hood. Kassie held Connor's hand.

He looked down at her. She was staring calmly at the Gulf, the clean two- to three-foot waves still swept by a light offshore breeze, the early afternoon water a deep emerald. There were salt crystals on her skin from evaporated seawater.

I gotta chill out, he thought to himself, remembering Maxim chatting her up in the water as they waited for more waves to come. Unlike the other guys, she actually seemed to have been listening to what Maxim was saying, and had even laughed a few times. Connor knew he should feel confident. She had practically told him that she was in love with him, and had practically invited him to study marine biology in San Diego so they could be together. Nevertheless, a persistent paranoia was trying to take over his thinking.

"It was perfect," Kassie said, unaware of Connor's doubt.

"Yes, yes it was," Connor answered. "Perfect Saturday. People will remember this for a long time."

Inside, though, Connor was feeling less than perfect. Sometimes he thought he'd seen Kassie discreetly eying Maxim, while other times she obviously was watching every move he made—and she seemed to like what she saw. Yet here they were, on the beach, his hand in hers. It felt as good and natural as Perfect Saturday's waves had been. But Connor knew Perfect Saturday was a one-off event. In his memory, there'd never been waves that good in Port Aransas. Ever.

Kassie nudged Connor's arm.

"Hey," she said. "I think Sandi is waving at us to come over to the fire."

Connor looked and saw Sandi motioning them to come

over to where the pier regulars had gathered. Maxim was holding his hands over the fire, Stamford was slamming a can of beer, and Franklin was talking with a bunch of the local guys, some of whom were good enough to beat the surfers from Corpus in the Gulf Coast Surfing Association contests.

"Come on," Kassie said, letting go of Connor's hand. "Let's go hang out with them."

Connor didn't want to; he knew what was coming. Whether indifferent or unaware, Kassie dropped her towel on the hood and strode toward the fire, and people already were turning to look her way.

Yeah. It'll always be like this, Connor thought, feeling suddenly vulnerable. *No one can take their eyes off her.*

Connor put his towel on the hood and slowly walked over to the fire, which was fueled by a few pieces of driftwood and scrap building material people had brought down to the beach. He saw the expressions on the guy's faces as they opened the circle to accept Kassie's arrival, and he knew what they were thinking.

Freaking jackals, Connor thought to himself as he followed Kassie. The circle closed around her before he arrived, though, blocking him out.

Maxim stood closest, jabbering at Kassie already, moving his hands as he described watching her catch and ride that first wave out at the fourth bar.

" 'No *way*,' " Connor heard, as Maxim described what he was thinking as he watched Kassie's ride. " 'She can't make that drop'—but then I was totally, 'Holy crap, she made the drop!'—and I was like, 'Dude, that chick can surf better than anybody out here!' I'm like, 'Who *is* that? Where did she learn to surf like that?' "

Stamford answered: "The North Shore, man. I thought it was bullshit, but I was wrong."

Other people spoke up, talking about what they'd seen, and how they watched her jump off the end of the pier and paddle straight for the fourth bar. Nobody mentioned Connor jumping off the pier with her.

"It's like, this girl isn't even wasting time on these piddly-ass five-foot waves at the end of the pier," Sandi said. "She's like, 'Gimme the big ones!'"

Rapid-fire comments followed quickly from the crowd:

"For real? The North Shore? You learned to surf on the North Shore?"

"When did you live there?"

"Did you know Gerry Lopez or Rory Russell?"

"What about Shaun or Rabbit?"

"Ben Aipa!"

"No, BK. BK!"

And so it went. At the back of the ring, Connor smiled and pretended to be paying attention to the banter, but he couldn't get close to Kassie without busting past some guys, which he thought would be rude—and weird. Not only that, but she also didn't even seem to be aware of him. It seemed like she was totally eating up all the attention—something he'd sensed at the Pod House. No one knew what she'd been up to with him for the last two weeks, including what had happened just a few days ago after seeing *Free Ride*, or about what she'd been telling him about her feelings.

Connor's mood went from totally stoked about the day's surf to a darkening nervousness, then to doubt, followed by simmering anger. He was tempted to walk back to his truck and drive home. But he knew that would be a fuck-up, so he stood his ground, determined not to seem nervous or jealous. Gradually, the comments between the guys started to turn competitive. They started to jockey for attention from Kassie, with Maxim supreme, touching Kassie's arm at times in an obviously flirtatious way. But after a few minutes of it, Kassie started to tell people she needed to go home.

"I'll give you a ride."

"No, I will."

"Clearly," said Jimmy, one of the best surfers in Port Aransas, "I mean, clearly, she wants *me* to give her a ride."

He tried to move in toward her and put his arm around her waist, but she sidestepped and swept his arm away from her with martial-arts finesse.

Everyone laughed.

"Oh, no, thanks. I've got a ride," she said, pointing over at Connor. "He's my ride."

All the guys looked at Connor. Some seemed amused, while others displayed looks of disbelief and envy.

"This was the best day of waves I've ever seen in Texas," Kassie said. "I mean, like *Surfer* magazine-quality waves—and just a few of us out, too. None of the crowds you get in Cali or Hawaii, and none of the bullshit localism. We had it all to ourselves. God bless this forgotten shore."

For a moment, there was silence, like some kind of revelation had been given.

"This forgotten shore," Maxim murmured. Then he raised his beer up: "Hell, yes, my friends, I'll drink to that. To the forgotten shore!"

Kassie said goodbye to everyone, and the circle of jackals reluctantly parted to let her join Connor. Together, they walked toward Connor's truck, but inexplicably she did not take his hand or show any sign of affection toward him. That irked Connor. They got in his truck, he fired it up, and they pulled away without speaking.

The fire crackled and the surfers stood around talking, drinking their beers while they watched the surf going flat.

TWENTY-TWO

DRIVING DOWN THE BEACH, Connor and Kassie remained mostly silent. Kassie felt a prickly air coming from Connor, and that disturbed her. He seemed completely oblivious to how it made her feel when he hadn't stood beside her at the fire. He'd remained outside the whole group of people, glowering, when she'd wanted him right next to her, to help fend off the unwanted attention. His expression and body language made her think he was going to turn out to be one of the jealous types, who tried to completely control—and, thus, ruin—other people's lives, just like the way she had seen her uncle treat her Aunt Brenda, who was the real math genius of the family. Kassie's aunt was from a time when women didn't get scholarship offers for mathematics—and yet she *still* got scholarship offers. But then she got married to Alan, and he had shut down the college degree idea cold.

"That's not how this stuff works," Alan had told Kassie's aunt. "You think you can go out and be ogled by every man you work with? Nope. No way. *I* go out, and *I* earn the bread and butter. You can stay in the kitchen and raise the kids."

"Complete bullshit," muttered Kassie, not realizing she'd said it out loud.

"What?" said Connor, defensively. "You're saying it's bullshit that I'm pissed?"

"I wasn't thinking about you," Kassie said, then added: "Wait. You're pissed?"

In that moment, they drove past an ancient-looking man dressed like a hobo, pushing a lawnmower down the beach. He saw Kassie, his eyes bugged out, and he hooted and waved.

Kassie laughed.

"Who the hell was that?" she asked.

"Lawnmower Ted," Connor answered. "Look, Kassie, I guess I just don't understand."

"Understand what?"

"I mean, you let all these guys just flirt with you left and right. You don't even give any hint that you've been ... "

"Been what?" she interrupted.

Connor heard the ice in her voice, realized he might be saying the wrong thing at the worst possible time.

"I don't know," he said, completely missing the turn onto Sandcastle Drive that was a shortcut to the Sea Isle condos.

"You don't *know*?" she asked, incredulously. "I do. I do *know*. Didn't you just see that old guy? What'd you call him?"

"Lawnmower Ted."

"Did you see what Lawnmower Ted did when he saw me? You don't understand *that*?"

Connor swallowed an achy lump that had suddenly formed in his throat. He was a dumbass, and everything he wanted to say wound up being not what he actually said—or, sometimes worse, he actually did say what he wanted to say, like right now.

"I guess I just want things to keep going the way they have been," he said.

"You missed the turn," she said coldly, waving her arm back toward Sandcastle Drive.

"Sorry," he said, pulling a U-turn.

"I'm being stupid," he said. "I just wanted to stand there holding you. I didn't want all those other people to take you away from me."

"Ah," she said. "Maybe you should think a little bit beyond yourself, Connor. Did it occur to you that maybe I wanted you standing next to me? Did it occur to you that maybe I wanted all those guys to see that I was with you? You were acting like a sad little victim."

"Those guys were circling around you like jackals," he blurted out, not wanting to admit he'd lacked the guts to push past the few guys standing with their backs to him.

"So you noticed. Yeah, that happens to me all the time. How do you think that feels?"

Connor said nothing as Kassie waited in silence. He turned onto Sandcastle and drove slowly toward her condo, but he felt the pressure of her gaze, demanding an answer.

"Maybe you didn't notice," she said, reaching over and touching his hand, which was on the gear shift. "They all wanted to give me a ride home. They all claimed they were going to give me a ride home. And what did I tell them?"

Connor looked at her briefly, feeling incredibly stupid.

"You told them that you had a ride home already."

"That's right," she said. "And who did I leave with?"

"Me."

Kassie took her hand away from his, a withdrawal that he felt acutely.

Am I seriously going to fuck this situation up? he thought. *Ruin it?*

Neither said a word the rest of the way to her condo, which took no more than two minutes. But it felt like the longest, most unpleasant silence Connor had endured in his entire life. He pulled up at her place, stopped, turned the truck off.

"I'm sorry I didn't push my way past those guys to stand by you," Connor said. "That was weak."

Kassie breathed in the apology, then exhaled it. His admission that he'd made a silly mistake made her feel some hope after all.

"Sometimes you confuse me, Connor," she said. "I don't like to be confused. I don't like jealous people; they mess up other people's lives. I also don't like guys who have no self-confidence. You need to get past the doubts."

Her rebuke hit him hard, and for a moment he just sat still, staring out the front window.

But he knew he had to say something.

"I'm sorry," he said. "I just ... I haven't ever felt this way about a girl—a woman."

Kassie leaned forward, put her arms around his neck, started kissing him the way she had down at the beach a few nights before, after their date in Corpus. But they weren't at the beach now; they were at her condo, and she needed to go upstairs to get ready for dinner. She pulled back when the moment was right, put her hand on his cheek.

"I'm going to have an end-of-vacation party over here at the condo," she said. "A pool party. And you're the first one invited, so don't be acting all weird when other people show up. You know what guys do when they're around me, and you have to be able to handle it."

"It's not you, it's ... "

"Kassie!" they heard her mom yelling down from the balcony above.

"Oh, shit, it's my mom," Kassie said, laughing. "I bet she saw me kissing you."

She grabbed her towels and her extra T-shirt, then scooted over by the door.

"Connor, that was so much fun. I want to surf with you. With *you*, OK?"

"I promise I won't weird out on you anymore."

"Good," she said.

"Kassie Her-NAN-dez!" her mom yelled again. "Get up here and help get dinner ready. Your dad's waiting!"

"Jeez," Kassie said, rolling her eyes. "You'd think I was nine years old or something."

She squeezed his hand.

"I'll call you tomorrow."

TWENTY-THREE

CONNOR STOPPED his truck in a spot right next to the harbor breakwater and got out. A short but wide wooden dock stretched into the murky-green harbor water, with a small, rusty utility crane folded up on the breakwater. The crew boat *Jayne Mansfield* was tied up here, the rubber tires around its gunwales squeaking as it rocked gently against the dock. Connor saw Stamford moving around inside the pilothouse. He'd come to fill out the forms to work as Stamford's deckhand.

The boat was a sixty-footer, with a gray hull and white superstructure. There were two orange lifeboats on top of the crew cabin area, a bunch of antennas on top of the bridge, and a small radar dome. Connor was getting excited as he stepped onboard; he walked over the rough wood decking to the crew cabin hatch and pulled it open. But it was way heavier than he thought, and he had to put some muscle into it. He stepped inside, and it slammed shut behind him, the long door handle whacking him solidly on his lower back.

"Ah, jeez!" he cried out in pain.

Stamford called from up front. "That you, Connor? You OK?"

"The damn door just stabbed a big hole in my back," he answered.

"Gots to pay attention on the *Jayne Mansfield*, bro," Stamford said. "This girl bites."

He poked his head down from the starboard-side bridge staircase.

"Ready for your tour?" he asked Connor, smiling and holding out a joint he'd just rolled.

Connor laughed.

"Do they have any idea you get stoned on board, you cretin?"

"Ah, hell, they don't look into that shit, long as the job's getting done," Stamford said. "Good pay, good food. Best job in Port Aransas."

They met halfway down the crew cabin. It was coated white inside with heavy enamel marine paint, a linoleum floor, and linoleum-topped dining tables down each side of the boat. Red vinyl covered the bench seating that surrounded each table. It looked like they had been taken straight out of a diner from the sixties.

After lighting up and taking a quick hit, Stamford motioned Connor to follow him.

"I'll show you your domain," he said. "It's all yours, like the wheelhouse is mine."

At the front of the crew cabin, they descended some stairs down into the galley, which Connor was surprised to notice was slightly bigger than the biggest kitchen in his dad's hotel cottages. Stamford motioned him over to the fridge.

"Check this out, bro," he said, and yanked open the door.

It was stocked with all kinds of junk food and sodas—and even some illicit beer.

"Strictly after-hours supplies," Stamford said. He raised his eyebrows, making like a manager type.

"Man, we got steak down here, cheese, chips, salsa, plenty of frozen fish, and even shrimp, crab—and every once in a while, they even have lobster on the requisition sheets."

"Wow," Connor said.

"Yeah, basically you just go down this big list. It's the same company that supplies the restaurants. You check off the item and it shows up the next time the delivery truck comes. No questions asked."

"I could dig that," Connor said.

"We don't run crews out very often," Stamford said. "Most of the time we take parts and victuals to the roughnecks on the rigs. They eat plenty of steak too, let me tell you—and ice cream. We keep the beer on board for when they get picked up after a two- or three-week stint. Them roughnecks—and the engineers too—they're ready to start partying. I've been known to share a toke with one or two of them sometimes on the way back in."

"How much did you say it pays?"

"I think I can get seventeen-fifty for you to start. Only goes up from there."

"Damn, man, I shoulda been doing this the last two years. I'd be driving something different than that Toyota pickup truck," Connor said.

"Damn straight," Stamford answered. "That's the spirit. If you want in, I just gotta have you fill out the application form. My boss brought one over the last time he was out. Don't misspell anything, though. It's the only one I got!"

Connor sat down at one of the aluminum-trimmed linoleum tables and filled out the form carefully, thinking of all the dollars he was soon going to be putting in his pocket. Maybe new wheels for his truck were finally on the menu.

Pelican's was busy as hell in the summer, and he'd always thought he made good money there. The best he ever seemed to do on busy nights was a comparatively measly thirteen to fourteen bucks an hour. And that was on a good night. Pelican's closed once the wintertime tourist doldrums set in, so he was out of work there after Labor Day.

After filling out the application, Stamford took him to the other parts of the boat and described the work Connor would have to do. Mostly, it sounded like hanging out doing a lot of nothing. Sometimes he'd have to sleep on the boat, but the bunks seemed to be pretty comfortable.

Connor had been twenty-fifth out of the 125 in his high school graduation class. He had earned lots of Cs, and had less-than-impressive SAT and ACT scores. But that wasn't even on his mind. He was tired of school, even if he read a lot on his own about marine mammals like the bottlenose dolphins and orcas in the books Franklin's dad let him borrow. If he could save some money, he'd go see Kassie in Midland this fall, before she started the spring semester at UC San Diego in January. If that went well—and he barely allowed himself to think it—then maybe he could move to Cali. The more money he saved now the better.

Once Stamford showed him around the boat they went outside to the foredeck where Stamford smoked a full reefer and Connor drank one of the beers "reserved" for the rig crew.

"There's an unlimited supply of that," Stamford said when Connor asked if he could have a another.

"So," Stamford said. "You seem to be spending a lot of time with Kassie."

"Maybe a little," Connor answered, determined to keep his experiences to himself. The last thing he wanted was to take a ribbing from Stamford.

"Doctor Love?" Stamford asked.

"Oh, my God," Connor said.

Stamford laughed.

"Go ahead. Keep your secrets. I think you've been laying pipe with her, though."

"I don't kiss and tell," Connor said.

Stamford whacked him on the shoulder.

"It's about damned time," he said to Connor. "Anyway, I knew it. And now you've just told me without actually telling me. Man, you're a lucky mofo. There's not one dude on this island that's laid eyes on her that isn't talking about asking her out. Maxim can't figure out the spell you cast on her, either—but he's working on his own magic."

Connor was unhappy about this talk—and didn't like the idea of going up against Maxim for Kassie's attention.

"You're fucking with me," Connor said. "Always and ever."

"That's why you love me, bro," Stamford said. "Anyhoo, we'll see, my friend. We'll see soon enough. You know she asked everyone at the shop to go to her party, right? I mean, she told you about that, didn't she?"

Connor smiled.

"First to know," he said. "She said some of her friends from Midland are coming down. She said three of them were cheerleaders, and another had been voted most beautiful junior at her school."

Stamford cocked his head.

"Most beautiful?" he said. "Shit, I gotta see that. I mean, if Kassie says that? Damn."

"I'm sure you guys will have plenty to keep you busy," Connor said.

TWENTY-FOUR

KASSIE'S DAD took her to Galveston and Houston for a couple of days to see some old friends at NASA. When they got back, the day before her pool party, she called Connor on the phone.

"I'm missing you," was the first thing she said.

"I'm ready right now," he told her.

"Mmm," she said. "Listen, baby, my friends are coming in from Midland today, and I promised them we would all go out to Corpus together to the mall. No boys."

"What? That's not fair."

"We need privacy to make our plans," she said. "Also, everyone at Geri's Surfboard Shop said they'd be coming to the pool party when I told them about it. They were stoked that my beauty contest-winning friends were going to be there."

"Stamford mentioned that," Connor said. "He has designs on all of them—and I won't be surprised if he succeeds. By the way: I'm gonna work on his boat as a deckhand."

Kassie was silent for a moment.

"You're sure?" she asked. "Isn't that dangerous work?"

Connor heard the disappointment in her voice.

"I mean, it's just for now," he said. "I mean, it's good money—and the more I save, the better for when I decide to go to school. Anyway, it's probably safer than, say, working in the oilfields in Midland."

Again, Kassie didn't respond. Connor disliked the silence.

"I mean," he said, almost not wanting to ask, "does that make you mad?"

"We should talk about it," Kassie said.

"About what?" he asked.

"Oh, come on, Connor," she said. "About what you're going to do. You know, like what you're going to do with the rest of your life."

"Haven't I got at least a little bit of time to think about that?" he asked.

"No."

"You're putting me under pressure!" he said, laughing.

"It's only fair," she replied. "You had me under pressure the other night. Your body, pressing right down on top of me. Hard."

"Hard?"

"It felt right, didn't it?" she asked.

"Why, whatever do you mean?"

Kassie laughed, then said: "You know exactly what I mean. If it weren't for the helicopter ... "

Connor's heart raced.

"Don't say that," he said. "I'll come over right now."

"I'm alone."

"Don't tease me like this, Kassie Hernandez."

She laughed again.

"Listen to me," she said. "Don't you even dare think about flirting with my girlfriends. They're all on my team, and they'll have their eyes on you, Connor O'Reilly. They'll be *watching you*."

"Spies! Talk about jealous people—"

She cut Connor off, laughing again.

"Now I'm going to hang up on you," she said. "What do you think about that?"

Connor didn't waste the opening.

"I think if you're really alone, but you're not going to let me come over, then you should at least be spending some quality time in your bedroom thinking of me,"

"Maybe I will," she whispered. "In fact, I know I will. Bye."

Before he could say anything, Connor heard the click of the receiver being clamped down on the cradle of the phone, then the warm, electric buzz of the dial tone.

―――――

The phone rang again a few minutes later. Connor snapped it up, hoping Kassie was calling back, but it was Stamford.

"Hey, man, I know you aren't supposed to start until after Kassie leaves, but I wanna see if you can help me out today. I have to go out on a quick run to a rig: easy in, easy out. It'll only take about four hours, but I'll write you in for eight if you'll do it."

"Sure," Connor said. "Kassie's busy all day with her girlfriends."

"All right, man. Get down here as soon as you can."

Connor put on some jeans and his Adidas, left a note for his dad, then he hopped in his truck and drove to the harbor.

Stamford was already warming up the diesels when he

got there, light black smoke and heat wavelets shimmering from out of the stacks. Connor parked and got out, walked out on the dock and hopped on the boat, went through the cabin door up to the bridge.

"Hey, man," Stamford said. "Thanks for helping out. I need to deliver some boxes of food to a crew on the rig *Elle Dean*, about ten miles out."

"It's light swell today," Stamford said, "which is good. Wouldn't want you to have to deal with big waves out there right off the bat."

"Sure," Connor said.

Stamford pointed at the stern, then the bow.

"Untie us, dude. We got victuals to deliver."

"All right, boss man," Connor said, watching Stamford work the controls. It seemed pretty cool to be operating a boat this size. Connor had only ever run a twenty-two-foot fishing boat, which had been fun. But this was the real deal.

"Get on them ropes," Stamford said. "We gotta go."

Connor went out through the crew cabin hatch onto the clear deck, jumped over onto the dock, ran up to the bow, untied the thick rope from the dock cleat. He tossed the rope on board. Then ran down to the stern, untied that rope too, threw it onto the deck, then jumped back aboard. The fact that the clear-deck gunwale was no more than six inches high off the deck struck him as a really good idea, as having to climb over a waist-high railing would be a pain. On the clear deck, he coiled the stern rope like the one on the starboard side. It was three inches thick, and heavy.

Could cut my arm off if I got it caught in a coil and the rope suddenly yanked tight between the boat and a rig, he thought.

With the *Jayne Mansfield* untied, Stamford eased her away from the dock into the glassy green water of the harbor.

The boat swung into a turn that pointed it toward the exit, and Stamford—really smoothly, Connor noticed—put the boat briefly in neutral, then into forward gear. Foam gently bubbled up behind the stern, fizzing like a soda poured into a glass with ice. They started heading out, sliding past the row of boathouses that lined the south side of the harbor, then past Uncle Jack's place, where Connor saw the big Hatteras that Uncle Jack owned—the one that his son Ben, who was in Connor's class during high school, had used as a Playboy-style sex pad. Many a bawdy, drunken night had been spent by Connor and his other friends at Uncle Jack's when Ben threw his wild-ass parties. In fact, Connor had almost lost his virginity there one night when he was fifteen—but it wasn't something he liked to remember because of how things had turned out. Stamford had snuck into the cabin with Toni when Connor had gone to find a condom. By the time Ben had given him one and he had hurried back to the boat, the door to the lower cabin was locked. When he'd banged on it and called Toni's name, Stamford's loud voice had answered: "She's busy."

Connor wondered if Stamford even remembered that particular escapade—or if Toni did, for that matter. She'd moved away a few weeks later, so he'd never had another chance with her.

As Stamford guided the boat out of the glassy harbor, Connor busied himself coiling the remaining ropes and making sure everything was tidy and ready for the coming work in the Gulf.

———

The twin diesels of the *Jayne Mansfield* droned. The smell of diesel billowed past Connor in a thin veil, the bow splash raged as the crew boat rose and fell in the gray-green sea. His T-shirt flapped against his taut body in the wind as he grasped a handhold at the rear of the crew deck, thrilled on his first day as a deckhand.

When they got to the rig, Stamford gave straightforward instruction: "Put the goods in the net, attach the net to the crane hook, then get the fuck out of the way!"

On the back deck, it was a wild moment for Connor. The wood-planked deck pitched in the four-foot swell. There was an identifiable rhythm: Far above, he saw the crane operator enter the control cabin, then the girded arm swung over the boat, a giant tackle block dropping quickly down. Connor backed away even farther; the block was twice the size of his head and made of solid steel. It was hanging perfectly still—but because of the pitching movement of the deck, it appeared to be swaying all over the place. It was like a wrecking ball ready to bash his brains out.

Connor heard Stamford shouting.

"Don't try to catch hold of the tackle! It'll jerk you right off the deck when the next swell comes."

Connor never thought his skills as a surfer would come in handy on the job.

For a moment, Connor watched; then, on a swell drop, he rushed forward, grabbed the net loop, and crouched next to the boxes of groceries loaded in the net. He was waiting for the next swell to jack the boat deck skyward again. The tackle hovered ten feet above his head, then the swell arrived, and the back end of the boat rose. Connor reached for the tackle's hook, almost had the supply net loop on it when the net went taut, and he couldn't get it on the hook.

The boat deck dropped as the swell passed, the crane tackle rose out of reach.

Connor readjusted his position and waited.

On the next swell the tackle dropped down to chest height. He reached in fast, slapped the loop over the heavy crane hook and jumped back. The boat dropped away, and the net stretched upward with the tackle. Connor scrambled away, raised both arms skyward, signaling the crane operator to reel the net up to the rig.

The supplies in the net rose quickly. Connor could see a couple of guys about thirty feet up on the platform waiting to snatch the goods. To him, it looked exactly like the nets that they had used to lift the Apollo astronauts from the sea into the helicopter after splashdown.

While Connor was distracted, Stamford hit the gas. The twin diesels roared, a fan of water sprayed out, white foam rooster-tailed high in the air. Connor lurched to keep his balance as the boat shot away from the rig.

TWENTY-FIVE

PARTY TIME.

Connor got into his truck and drove down Eleventh Street to the Sea Isle condos. He turned onto its winding asphalt drive, his truck leaning precariously with each curve. Then he braked hard and pulled into the parking area for Kassie's unit.

Nary an open spot.

Connor had to park at the next building over. He got out, walked to where the action was, his flip-flops slapping loudly against the bottoms of his feet. He was in top gear, totally stoked. He'd had two beers before even coming over, because that seemed to make him somewhat reckless, and he'd finally noticed that while Kassie liked different parts of his nature at different times—she was deeply attracted to him when he showed a fearless confidence in their relationship.

He heard the party when he got out of his truck: music, people screeching, a big splash at the pool and a lot of laughter. He headed to the stairs and bounded up two and three at a time to the door, opened it without knocking, went in.

Kassie's condo was packed. It looked like the whole town had shown up, including the surf shop crowd, all of Connor's friends, the older surfers, barflies, and the walking, talking, semi-employed fishing bums. Dudes circled around what must have been Kassie's friends—*like jackals circling prey*, thought Connor. *Of course, was he really any better?*

Connor saw Franklin and Robinson, each holding beers, standing alone in a corner, ever observing, gawking, but never making a move. Connor snatched a Lone Star from an ice chest on the kitchen table, went to them.

"Well now," he said. "Busy trying to get laid, are we?"

"Eh, fuck you, Connor," Robinson said. Before he could complete what he had to say, though, both Franklin and Connor simultaneously said what always came next: "I oughta kick your ass."

Robinson laughed.

"Cheers," Connor said, raising his Lone Star. "Maybe you really should kick my ass, Robinson. It may be your last chance. I might just be leaving this forgotten shore."

"What are you talking about?" Franklin said. "Stamford says you're his deckhand. You think you're gonna drown out there or something?"

"Hah. No, I mean maybe I might be taking a 'surfari.' Maybe I'll head out west."

"Eh?" Robinson squeaked. "What are you talking about, Connor?"

"I mean that after saving up some coin, I might just go to Cali for some waves."

"What?!" Franklin exclaimed. "You mean you'd abandon your old man here alone to run the cottages? You are a bastardly fuck, aren't you?"

"A true bastard bitch, I guess," Connor said. He took a swig, then another, trying to chill the burn in his chest Franklin's unexpected comment had ignited. He hadn't thought about leaving his dad here alone. His dad, who was already starting to drink way too much. His mom was somewhere, her last whereabouts in Colorado. He surveyed the crowd while taking a couple more big swigs of beer.

"Anybody seen Kassie?" he asked, casually.

"Kassie?" Robinson replied. "Last I saw, she was down by the pool."

Kassie had been working the crowd. It was something she liked to do at parties—especially because if she stayed put too long, she'd soon be surrounded. In fact, she tried to stay on the other side of the pool from Maxim, who seemed to never give up. Sandi wasn't around, and Maxim kept looking at her. He'd taken off his shirt, was bare-chested, bare-footed, dressed only in white linen pants that had a drawstring. Kassie could make out surf baggies under them—and it appeared that something Sandi had told her might be true. His hip lines and six-pack abs, his strong pecs and perfect biceps, his steely eyes and tight curly hair presented a striking vision: He seemed the incarnation of Poseidon, god of the sea. Kassie thought of how the Greek gods would sometimes appear to some human victim they wanted to have sex with, emerging from a shroud of mist while presenting themselves as perfection in the eyes of their prey. That was Maxim. And there was no denying that he was the hottest guy at the party, looks-wise. He was also a very simple man: no jealousy, no complicated emotional life. He saw, he wanted, he took.

He'd pound me like a beast, she thought.

She also knew he'd drop her the next morning, with no qualms and no regrets—certainly with no remorse. He would go right back to Sandi's bed as soon as he wanted her comfort. Sandi, for her part, actually seemed to encourage him. She liked that he was irresistible, and maybe that proved to her that he was worth keeping.

No doubt it was all the margaritas she'd been drinking that fired her superficial appreciation of Maxim. It occurred to her that Connor would be incensed if she acted on the vague impulse in her head. He'd certainly be so angry—and jealous—that he would either break up with her on the spot or behave in a way that would justify her breaking up with him. That would be awful, and the thought made her heart ache. But the evil girl within her that came to life with alcoholic stimulation whispered anyway: *If you do Maxim it would solve all kinds of problems.*

Poseidon could send her off to California unencumbered and free.

Kassie kept looking over to the pool gate to see if Connor had arrived yet, but she saw no sign of him. She didn't know why he hadn't been the first to arrive. It made her feel bad and a thought popped into her head: *What if he was the one being a two-timer? What if he has a girlfriend he hasn't told me about?*

She didn't like that thought at all. For a brief moment, she acknowledged in her heart that when someone was in love, jealousy was a simple, real thing. Maybe an unavoidable thing.

One margarita after the next, the heat had started to build until Kassie's friend Alex declared it was just too damned hot for the pool to be empty. She downed her drink, stripped out of her T-shirt and miniskirt, kicked her flip-flops away, and dove into the deep end right next to the "No Diving" sign. Alex popped up, smiling, treading water while she arranged her long blond hair with one of the many ponytail holders she had around her wrist.

"So?" Kassie asked.

Alex took a look around the pool. Every guy there had turned to look at her, a girl in a red bikini cooling off in the shimmering light-blue water.

"So what the hell are y'all waiting for?" said Alex. "This feels *great!*"

Rapid-fire splashes quickly followed as men and women jumped into the pool from all sides. Kassie's friend Becky appeared with a tray of plastic shot cups and called out: "Tequila shots! Jell-O tequila shots! Pick your color!"

People swarmed her.

Stamford was standing next to Maxim by the gate.

"Tequila shots," he said, deadpan. "That's when the panties drop."

Maxim grinned.

"Can't say I've ever needed to rely on that, Stamford. But to each his own."

"Yeah, well, the bet's still out there, isn't it? And right now I'm winning—gonna win, too, because Kassie's leaving in a couple days."

They watched Kassie at the other side of the pool as she casually stripped down to her low-cut bikini with a string top. She was flawless. She looked over at them and kept her eyes on them as she walked slowly down the cement steps into the water while holding the chromed rail, looking like Venus submerging. In slow motion, she leaned forward into the water. Then she breast-stroked over their way, toward the deep end. She stopped and began treading water, looking directly at Maxim.

"Well, aren't you gonna come?" she asked.

TWENTY-SIX

CONNOR FINISHED off his Lone Star and considered getting another. Franklin was talking about Perfect Saturday just a week ago, when he had almost pulled off a vertical off-the-lip 360. He and Robinson had seen Connor get his barrel ruined by Stamford, had seen Kassie wowing everyone with her incredible surfing. Her talent stoked them all. And yet, on the beach, all the dudes wanted to do was lay her down and stick themselves into her. *Forget the surf girl, take the goddess,* Connor thought as he unconsciously crunched the empty beer can in his hand.

"Y'all need another beer?" he asked.

They said yes, and Connor retrieved. They cracked the beers open and tossed the tabs into a nearby trashcan.

Robinson talked about getting sucked over the falls and being trapped inside.

"I remember that," Franklin said. "I was laughing my ass off, just like that time you sank the skiff."

"Eh, I oughta kick your ass for bringing that up," Robinson said—but he laughed at the skiff memory too.

Franklin recalled: Once, when they were all drunk at Jim Powell's place, Robinson had come up with a scheme to take his skiff to St. Jo's. They'd go around the north jetty and go in to where the waves were starting to break. They wouldn't have to use the Jetty Boat, walk across St. Jo's, or even paddle out, because they would switch out manning the skiff, keep it outside the lineup, and surf. When they ran out of beer and weed they'd head back.

It was cold in the skiff on the way over to St. Jo, swell five to six feet going around the tip of the north jetty. Moments later, they were piling out of the skiff just outside the third sandbar: Franklin, Connor, and Ron Castle, who had brought a three-finger bag of weed. Robinson took the first shift in the skiff.

The waves sucked, but they all caught some about the same time, and moments later were all paddling back out through the chop. When they were close to where the waves were breaking again, they saw Robinson standing at the back of the skiff, gunning the motor, a wild look on his face. The skiff was charging into a medium-sized wave that had suddenly jacked up behind it. The back of the skiff lifted up high, the bow of the skiff pointed down—and it plunged straight under the water.

The bow hit bottom, the boat stopped cold, and Robinson was ejected. Whitewater swamped over the skiff, tossing everything out. The ice chests burst open and immediately there were beer and soda cans, bags of sandwiches and potato chips, bobbing all around in the seawater. At first, they laughed incredulously. Then they heard Castle's wild cry: "The weed! The weed, you idiot! The weed!"

Robinson clambered back aboard the skiff, sitting up to his belly in water, one hand on each gunwale of the swamped boat, trying to keep it from turning over. He was grinning at his own foolishness.

Connor laughed repeatedly as Franklin continued the tale.

The boys beached the skiff and bailed it out, while Franklin had to walk half a mile just to get to the Jetty Boat dock, wait for it, and then walk to the Coast Guard station to ask for help. Hours later, a small cutter showed up, and the skiff got towed back to Port Aransas harbor.

"That sucked," Connor said. "I almost freaking drowned when I paddled out to the cutter. They lowered a rope for me, but I could barely hang on. I thought I was a goner."

Robinson grinned.

"Eh. I guess it's funny now," he said. "But I lost a lot of money that day."

Connor saw a commotion in the kitchen, saw Kassie's friend Becky carrying a tray of Jell-O shots out the door down toward the pool. While she was passing through the room, people tried to pick shots off the tray.

"No chance," she said, laughing as she jerked the tray out of reach. "Pool party first!"

Franklin moved fast toward the door.

"May I?" he asked Becky as he opened the door for her.

"Why, thank you, sir," she told him.

"Maybe it's time to go down to the pool," Franklin said as he watched Becky descend the stairs.

They finished their beers and headed down to the pool.

There was a crowd at the bottom of the stairs snatching the tequila shots from Becky, and as they approached she offered.

"Shots," she said, pushing the tray at them. It wasn't a question.

Connor's friends each grabbed one, while he took two.

"Oh, so you're two-fisting," Becky said. "Well, bottoms up."

Robinson, Franklin, and Connor slammed their Jell-O shots. Franklin immediately turned away and spat red liquid against the wall, retching and coughing.

"Oh, man," he said. "That's awful!"

Becky frowned.

"Fail," she said.

She was so petite that she barely came up to Connor's chest. Kassie had told Connor that Becky was one of her best friends. She was beautiful, whip-smart, and had a sharp tongue she employed to embarrass people—especially boys she thought were cute. It was her come-on. And if a boy could handle it, then he had half a chance with her.

"You'd better stick to Lone Star," Becky said to Franklin, turning her nose up at the red goo oozing down the wall.

Connor and Robinson took the last of the Jell-O shots off her tray, then turned to thread their way through the breezeway to the pool.

"Becky," Franklin said, "I can't do Jell-O shots, but I'll take you on any day with straight tequila. You against me. I'll take you down."

"Oh, yeah?" she retorted. "Let's just see about that."

She grabbed Franklin's hand and led him up the stairs.

Connor smiled. Maybe Midland and Port Aransas just worked well together.

It took a little while to get to the pool area. They stopped a couple of times to talk surfing with some of their buddies. They were still stoked from their memories of Perfect Saturday.

Their friend Hilton said he'd seen a sand shark streaking through the top of a peaking wave. "Seemed like it was going ninety miles an hour," he said. "Freaked me out. I would have paddled in, but the waves were too good to be chased in by a three-foot sand shark."

Robinson and Connor emerged into the bright sunshine. The empty blue sky domed over the pool party, lots of people were standing around, a few were in the pool.

Robinson nudged Connor when they got to the pool's gate.

"Look," he told Connor. "Seems like Maxim's finally making a move."

Maxim knew Kassie had given him the opening he'd been waiting for. She'd watched as he'd stripped down to his Birdwell Beach Britches, watched as he'd lowered himself into the deep end, watched as he lunged forward into the water.

He breast stroked toward her, smiling.

"So this is what I saw," Maxim said when he got to her. "This crazy foxy lady jumps from the pier and paddles hard for the fourth bar, and then heads straight for a big-ass wedge building up, whips around, and does a better ride than anybody who lives in this town."

Kassie felt like blushing.

"Well, I dunno about that," she said.

"No shit. Really. Better than most the guys from Corpus I've surfed against in the contests. Where'd you learn?"

"O'ahu."

"No shit? Wow. Stamford says you knew some of the big names."

"Naw, just talked to them on the beach sometimes. They were cool. Maybe I picked up a lot watching. I was just a grom."

"Well, you're sure all grown-up now. Everybody on this island thinks you're the hottest thing on two legs."

"That's what I hear them say about you, too. Sandi says ..."

Kassie stopped herself. She couldn't believe she'd just said that to Maxim—and she didn't want to believe what she had been about to say to him.

Maxim moved a little closer. Unconsciously, Kassie backed up.

She looked around for support from her friend Alex, but she was across the pool next to Stamford, her chin resting on her forearms on the ledge of the pool. Stamford was sitting next to her, dangling his feet in the water as he talked. He must have clawed back some mojo, because she was laughing raucously at what he was saying. Stamford really was good-looking, but Connor was prettier. Then there was this guy, Maxim, and Kassie was starting to feel uncomfortable—like maybe she'd made a mistake being flirtatious.

Maxim kept pace with Kassie, who backed up until she bumped against the pool wall. Maxim came within slapping distance, but the water was too deep to stand where they were, so Kassie had her arms up over the pool edge, while Maxim was treading water.

"Sandi said what?" he asked. "Now I'm curious."

There was no way Kassie was going to repeat what Sandi said. It was not where she wanted the conversation to go, nor was this even a situation she wanted to be in. She didn't want to seem rude by jumping out of the water and walking around to the other side of the pool, but that was what she was about to do. It wasn't Maxim she wanted to have right in front of her right now.

Kassie found herself starting to tremble a little.

Maxim saw her quiver and interpreted it completely

wrong, thinking his mere presence was giving her shudders of desire.

"Sometimes Sandi exaggerates, but not always, if you know what I mean," he said.

Kassie frowned. It seemed like he knew what Sandi had told her. Maybe it was a setup.

"So let's go get some drinks before you leave town," he said. "I know a couple of good places in Corpus."

"Maybe so," she said. "But I'm pretty booked."

Maxim then put one of his arms out and grabbed hold of the pool edge, his thick biceps sculpted and tanned from surfing, and his triceps ... *nice,* Kassie thought. Maybe it was that third margarita that had gotten her in this position. Still, the urge to get away from Maxim got stronger, even if doing so would appear to be impolite.

Maxim saw her looking at his bicep, which was what he'd wanted.

"Like what you see?" he asked.

Kassie felt a surge of anger. *This guy is a joke!*

"Well, gee. I mean, what big muscles you've got. Right, Maxim?" she asked, as sarcastically as she knew how.

Maxim completely missed her insult.

He cocked his arm up, made a fist with his hand and flexed his bicep.

"You can touch it if you want," he said.

"Ooh, can I?" she asked, unable to resist making fun of him.

Kassie reached out and touched Maxim's bicep.

"It's so big and strong, Maxim," Kassie said, dripping every syllable with sarcasm and parody. "Just like Sandi said: You're so *big.*"

Maxim laughed, then moved right next to her. She instinctively recoiled, but the pool wall stopped her—and in that moment Kassie saw Connor standing at the gate, looking at her.

She watched him turn and walk away.

Kassie reacted violently, suddenly furious that Connor had seen what happened.

"Back off, man," Kassie said firmly to Maxim. "Back the fuck off!"

She knocked his arm away, raised her foot and planted it firmly on his sternum, shoved him away.

"Whoa!" said Maxim, surprised.

Kassie spun around, lifted herself forcefully out of the pool.

Maxim had no clue what was going on.

"Damn," he said as she rushed off. "That bitch is crazy."

TWENTY-SEVEN

CONNOR WAS ALMOST at his truck when he heard footsteps behind him, followed by Kassie's voice.

"Wait, Connor. What are you doing?"

He turned around and glared at her.

"I'm leaving."

"Connor, why? I've been waiting for you to get here all day."

"You know," he said, then stopped. He looked across the grassy dunes between the condo and Eleventh Street.

Kassie waited, and the silence was painful. It verified that he'd definitely seen her squeezing Maxim's bicep. She felt terrible because she had only jokingly egged Maxim on. She'd been backed into a corner by her own foolishness, and now this.

"I can explain," she said, trying to keep him there just a little longer. She was sure he'd understand.

Connor shifted on his feet uneasily, looking down, not taking in anything his eyes were seeing.

"I don't need you to explain," he said. "I don't want you

to explain. I thought we had something, Kassie. I got here an hour ago, but I wanted to give you space because I trusted you. I wasn't going to run around trying to track you down like I owned you or something. I came here to tell you something special. And then I see ..."

Connor fell silent and waved his arm while staring at the cement sidewalk.

"What did you see?"

"Oh, come on," he said, completely losing it. "I saw you with Maxim. I saw you getting up close and personal with that fucker."

"Connor, it's not true. I ... "

"You were laughing and smiling and grabbing onto him. Why do that to me, after what you said the other day?"

"It wasn't what it looked like, Connor," Kassie said, feeling guilty and scared—but also angry. Was he really going to do this?

"Aren't you even going to listen to me?" she asked, the alcohol making her aggressive.

"I don't need to," he said. "It's always the same thing with hot women. You're just like my mom!"

"Connor, what the hell are you talking about?"

"Are you crazy?! I oughta ask you the same question. You're the one feeling up Maxim in the pool. Nice arms, huh?"

"OK, that's enough," she said.

Kassie felt humiliated. Connor had seen her grab Maxim's arm, but he hadn't heard her sarcastic comments. He'd turned away before she'd shoved Maxim away from her. He hadn't seen her angrily get out of the pool. But here he was, acting exactly like the kind of guy she couldn't stand: Somebody who had no self-confidence at all, who was ridiculously jealous, and who would eventually tell her she needed to stay home, hidden away from life.

That got Kassie really mad. They'd talked about all this, and he'd said he wouldn't be jealous. And just as she was about to try again to explain nicely, the alcohol intervened—and the evil girl inside of her made her say something else.

"You know, Connor, I really believed you were the guy I was looking for," she said, glaring angrily at him. "I mean, I was about to tell you that we needed to find a way for you to come to San Diego. Fuck the crew boat work. But you know what? You're on the stupid crew boat with that moron friend of yours, Stamford. I think maybe you and Stamford deserve each other. I'll tell you one thing: Maxim doesn't deserve me—and he won't be getting me, either. What you saw in the pool was just part of what happened. But you don't seem to care about that—so I don't, either."

Drunken and infuriated, Kassie whirled around and started walking away.

Connor yelled after her: "A girl who can't even keep her hands to herself, and who jumps in bed with any guy who happens to look pretty? That's fine. I don't need any of that, either."

Kassie answered with a one-finger salute, not bothering to see its effect.

Completely pissed off, Connor got in his truck. He drove recklessly, punching the accelerator to the floor, then releasing it, pounding the wheel. He turned south on Eleventh Street, east on Sandcastle, driving as fast as possible until he got down to the beach. He parked and stared at the surf; once again, it was a washing machine of weak, brown lather.

"Jesus Christ," he said to himself, grabbing his head with his hands.

She had made out with him at the Pod House, but had then gone with Stamford to Pelican's—now he'd watched as she'd felt up Maxim's arm. And it seemed to please her. He had seen how Maxim had pressed up against her. Was he supposed to sit there and watch her make out with him, too? She had the same lack of control his mom had—and where was she?

Gone, he thought to himself.

The same pain he felt the day his dad had told him she was gone shot through him again.

"Screw this," he said. "Just screw this."

Then the destroyer inside of him stood tall, an inner voice that said: *You're a complete drunken fool. There was no way she was actually into Maxim. You must have misunderstood what was happening. She even said so. But you were too drunk and stupid to hear her. No way to undo your dipshittery now.*

He couldn't make the voice of self-hate and truth stop.

So how does it feel to have destroyed all this unbelievable beauty you were given?

Connor opened his truck door, vomited onto the sand.

TWENTY-EIGHT

KASSIE TRIED to listen to the baseball game with her dad, but it just wasn't working. There was a nagging feeling that she should do more, and that the situation with Connor could be patched up easy enough with a telephone call. But, for some reason, she wasn't doing it. Could the diploma she sought mean so much to her that she'd actually let Connor O'Reilly go?

The sweet AM radio broadcast of the game—so primitive and thin yet full of joy, tension, and excitement— just wasn't working its magic.

"I'm kind of tired, Dad," she said. "I think I'm gonna take a shower and crash out."

" 'Crash out' is a bad phrase in aeronautical engineering, Kassie," he said, trying to be clever.

She smiled at him. When Connor was good, he reminded her of her dad. When he acted like an idiot, he stirred feelings she had about her Uncle Alan.

Kassie yawned, then got up and kissed her dad on the cheek.

"I love you," she said.

"Love you, too."

She left the living room, abandoning the ritual that she'd so often shared with him since she was a gremmie on O'ahu. Usually only one of them being sick would stop them listening to the Astros play ball—and it *had* to be the Astros for an ex-NASA guy gone oilman. How much money they were pulling from the oil leases and well ownership, she didn't know. Maybe it was a lot, but her dad had been adamant that she needed to work hard in high school. She was required to get the best grades possible, to see if she could get a scholarship to one of the big engineering schools.

She had, and he was proud.

"It doesn't matter to me what university you go to," he told her, when the first scholarship offer had come in. "Women don't get a fair shake in engineering, or oil—hell, in any profession. I could pay for anything you want to do, but a scholarship to a good school would mean at least the professors might look at you as an equal to their male students. Let you play ball fair and square."

Play ball, she thought: Men were always trying to play ball with her. Always, ever—and his comments that so many wouldn't be fair to her at college were unnerving. But maybe he was right. Maybe the professors would be able to help her.

Kassie went upstairs to her room and let what was on her mind take her full attention as she laid on her bed. Was Connor one of those guys her dad talked about? Was he even worse, like her uncle, who believed a woman's place is in the kitchen? It still irritated her to think about the many times she'd heard her uncle say that.

Her Aunt Brenda might have gone to MIT and could have been working at NASA afterward with the likes of Margaret Hamilton, Poppy Northcutt, Katherine Johnson and the others. But, instead, exactly where was she right now?

In the kitchen.

"No freaking way," Kassie blurted out.

She put her pillow over her head and covered her eyes. She recalled that time in fourth grade when her teacher had been shocked to realize she could divide and multiply in her head, when other kids had barely learned to add and subtract.

"Where'd you learn this?" the teacher had asked. "Did your dad teach you?"

"No, ma'am," she replied. "He's good with math, but my mom and aunt can do it way better. Daddy says they're both geniuses. He says I got the counting gift from them."

Her dad also told her about Katherine Johnson's early work as a human computer at Langley that played an important role in Project Mercury—and the lunar missions that followed.

"You seem to have some things going on like Katherine did," her dad told her. "I wish I had the gift that you, your mom, and Aunt Brenda have."

Kassie felt those other women's stories were awesome. Nobody knew about them, and that was totally unfair.

Kassie rolled over and felt her lower belly aching, but her cramps were starting to go away.

She tried to sleep, but couldn't, so instead she tried to read a book on orbital mechanics she'd taken from her dad—yet not a single sentence got read before Connor would appear again in her head. Sometimes it was one those tense encounters, when all she could think about was raging desire: how it felt when his hands were on her, how he smelled like surfing, tasted salty clean, felt firm and smooth everywhere she touched.

Other times, she thought about the party, Maxim, the

fight. The worst part was that, deep in her heart, she knew she'd provoked Maxim. She was drunk. He was hot. The bad voice in her head seduced her to play. That wasn't fair to Connor, and she hadn't admitted that to him. His suspicions and anger weren't totally unfounded. But what if she'd told him that right then and right there?

She'd start the same paragraph in the book, again and again, but finally she snapped the book closed in frustration. It was hopeless.

She rolled up in her blanket.

"Connor," she muttered, face half-pressed into the mattress and half-covered by pillow, "I know in my heart you're not one of them."

She had an urge to go to the phone, pick it up, dial his number, and confess that she loved him. To apologize and admit she'd provoked Maxim, but also to make clear that he'd cornered her against her will. Thinking of doing that made her feel better. But before she committed to acting on her idea, the part of her protecting her dream spoke up: It was stupid of her to even be thinking about Connor. There were other guys and other loves. She was going to UC San Diego to study with a full scholarship, where she could surf the best spots in southern California. Connor, meanwhile, was going to be working on a crew boat in the Gulf of Mexico. She let that sink in: A crew boat in the Gulf. In reality they had nothing in common at all.

Was it really over? she thought.

"This is stupid," Kassie said aloud, refusing to give in. "I'll write him and explain."

She got up, went to her desk, got a pad of stationery and a pen.

TWENTY-NINE

"WE GOTTA TIE up at the standpipe," Stamford said. "The one you and me and Franklin scuba-dived a couple of years ago."

"Okay."

When they arrived Stamford backed the stern of the boat to within three or four feet of the platform, the diesels rumbling and thrashing as he would gun them either forward or reverse to keep the boat close. Connor had to loop a three-inch rope around his shoulder and dive off the rear of the boat. There was no time for doubt: Into the dark green he plunged. It was cold for a split-second, but by the time he splashed over to the leg of the standpipe he no longer noticed. His blurred vision revealed seaweed-draped barnacles and oysters as big as his hand, sharp as knives and packed tight. The loud, gurgling swell washed him forward and back, up and down, first toward the ladder rungs, then away from them. He had to time it perfectly. One more slosh and Connor lunged, grabbing a ladder rung with one free hand before putting his other hand on the rung below before the water sucked out. His bare foot found a rung below just as the water washed away.

He scrambled up and out of the way before the next swell had a chance to knock him back into the water. The stern of the boat bobbed up and down as a raw death threat; if he fell in now the propellers might suck him under and chop him to pieces. That thought made him climb fast. About fifteen feet up he reached the lower platform, the one designed for crew boats and other ships to tie up to. He stepped onto the platform through the open gate at the leg, then made a double half-hitch around the railing that would hold the boat to the platform.

Stamford had done a great job keeping the *Jayne Mansfield* in position. Watching from the platform, Connor realized he was exhausted.

Stamford gunned the motors, doing his best to keep the boat almost exactly on the standpipe without going under it or bashing into the legs. The engine's roar, the foam shooting from the spinning propellers, was scary. When a swell went past the clear deck was a scant five to eight feet below; a trough put it fifteen feet below. Connor had to time his jump perfectly, then hit the deck and roll, or screw it up and possibly break a leg. Worst of all he might fall in the water between the standpipe and the boat and get crushed against the barnacles and oysters.

Stamford was waving at him to jump.

Connor climbed over the railing, held on with both hands while leaning out, and when the boat was almost at the top of a swell, he jumped.

―――

Kassie's mom shouted up the stairs a few moments after picking up the phone.

"Hey, dear," she said. "Andrew is on the phone. He wants to talk to you."

Oh, God, Kassie thought.

Andrew had played quarterback for Midland their senior year, while Kassie had been captain of the dance team. They had been voted homecoming king and queen. It seemed to the whole school that they were the classic high school sweethearts who would date all four years, get married after graduation, and live the rest of their lives together in the oilpatch. Andrew would be running oilfields, Kassie would be raising kids.

"No way," Kassie murmured.

"Babe?" her mom said. "What did you say?"

"Hang on, Mom. I'll pick up in a sec."

She went to the hall phone and picked up.

"Hello?"

"Hi Kassie," Andrew said. "I've missed you."

"Oh ... yeah. Well, yeah. So, what have you been doing since graduation?"

"My dad took me on a trip to Wyoming to visit his brother. He owns a giant cattle ranch up there. My uncle was trying to get me to come up there and help him out. He said he needed a man to help him run the place since his daughters were going to get married someday and not be able to help him anymore."

"He said that? What did his daughters say? Did he ask them about it?"

"What? His daughters?" Andrew asked, confused. "I mean, they were all pretty and everything but I don't think they'd have much to say about running a ranch. Didn't really think to ask them."

"When do you think you'll go up to Wyoming?"

"I don't know. I reckon there's a girl here in Midland I might want to ask about that."

"Who's that?"

Kassie could hear the faint hum of the phone line.

"I mean, well ... so, I guess maybe you had a good time at the coast?"

"Sure. Maybe too much fun. But at the same time maybe not quite enough."

"Oh. I guess that sounds pretty good."

"Listen, Andrew, my dad is needing me to come down and look some stuff over about my scholarship."

"So I guess your heart is set on San Francisco?"

"San Diego."

"Wherever the Golden Gate is, yeah. Well, I'll let you go. But I want to get together soon and talk about my trip to Wyoming. I bet you'd really love it up there."

"Yeah," Kassie said. "I bet it's a great place to visit."

———

Nothing was happening while the boat pitched and rolled for hours next to the standpipe. Stamford had said they might get called to a rig to pull some guy off who was ill, but another boat was loading up to go out there. Or the guy might get so sick that they'd have to call a chopper. There also was a chance they'd get called to Port Isabel. So they were going to stay put because management didn't want to waste diesel going back to Port Aransas.

The boat heaved, it sloshed, it jerked hard against the heavy rope Connor had tied to the standpipe. It rolled and pitched and yawed and bounced.

Above them was a cloudless azure sky, an indifferent sun beating down.

Connor felt his insides slithering around like they were trying to erupt out of his mouth. He couldn't find a place to be in the boat that helped: Not the bunks below the bridge, not on the bridge, not in the crew cabin, not out on the clear deck. He tried smoking a reefer with Stamford, who felt sorry for him. Stamford told Connor that, for some people, smoking weed made the seasickness go away. But the joint didn't provide any relief.

"I mean, maybe you should take some Lone Star out of the fridge," Stamford said. "Let it get nice and hot, then open it and slug some down. If you just threw up, you'd feel better."

Connor lay down on the café-like booth seats in the crew cabin trying to keep his eyes closed, but the sensation of needing to throw up and yet being unable to actually do it was made worse by lying on his back.

The swell was getting more intense, making the boat tilt and jump. The wind whipped, diesel fumes permeated everything. Connor inhaled deeply, hoping the toxic smell would make him finally blow beets. But that didn't work, either. On his back, he watched the curtains over the window, swaying first this way, then that way, then this way, then that. He heard the metal clips clap against the window. Over and over they clapped on the windows until the whole world was colored green. He remembered Kassie turning away and flipping him off, his dad crying when his mom had left them.

Abruptly he felt the contents of his stomach were going to burst out, now—*right now!*

He tumbled down to the head, yanked the door open and let fly into the toilet. He hurled loudly and with no shame, sounding like a dinosaur being disemboweled by a gigantic sword.

Up on the bridge he heard Stamford hoot.

"Let it go, Connor. Let it go!"

Connor gagged when no more would come, breathing like he'd run a marathon. The awful sensation of nausea relented swiftly; he grabbed a towel and wiped his face, ran water in his mouth and spit it out. He flushed the can again and Stamford hooted more.

"Hell yeah," Stamford hollered. "Flush it out. Flush it *out!*"

He peered down from the bridge, leaning over the edge of the port stairwell.

"How ya doin', buddy?"

There were tears in Connor's eyes.

The sour taste was still powerful in his mouth, along with the sting in his nostrils, and the boat was still lurching impolitely—but now he felt clear and clean. He spit into the basin again, wiped his eyes, and looked up at Stamford.

"I'm good."

"It only takes once, brother. You won't get that sick ever again."

The radio crackled, and Stamford disappeared.

Connor cleaned up the head, then went to the fridge, where he grabbed two Lone Stars. Then he made his way up to where Stamford was.

"Here," he said. "To my newly gained sea legs."

Stamford eyed the Lone Star. He knew he wasn't supposed to drink now, but ...

"Fuck it," he said, and took the can.

They cracked them open, put the tabs in the dashboard ashtray, and guzzled.

"You know something?" Stamford said, wiping beer foam from his mouth.

"What?"

"That time last summer. What do you call it? Perfect Saturday?"

"Yeah."

"I'm sorry I ruined that tube ride for you, man. But, I mean, I was so freaked out. You looked so cool in that tube, so like a picture in a magazine—like a surfer wrapped in a North Shore barrel, like maybe at Log Cabins or even Off-The-Wall."

"Really?"

"Really. It was like *Free Ride*, dude," Stamford said. "I was mesmerized. I wanted you to go past me in slow motion in the tube, like Tomson does in the movie. But you bailed before you got to me. I felt awful. But I'll never forget that vision of you in the tube, man. Never."

THIRTY

KASSIE FELT LIKE SHIT. She was slumped on the couch, gazing at the TV without paying any attention to the M*A*S*H rerun. The remote control was in her hand, but she didn't change the channel. She should be excited. She was about to reap the reward of four years of hard studying and many years more dreaming about what she wanted her life to be. Instead she was mad. Disappointed. And it wasn't Connor's fault. It was *hers*. She hadn't written to him; she hadn't summoned the courage to call him. It was total radio silence from her, and he didn't deserve that.

She put her head in her hands.

"No," she said.

"No what?" her mom asked.

Kassie looked up and saw that her mom had been watching her from the entrance to the TV room. No telling how long she'd been spying. Her mom said nothing further but moved over toward the couch and sat next to her.

"Listen, I know when my baby's not right," her mom said. "You've been in a funk since we left the coast."

"I don't want to talk about it, Mom."

"So," her mom said. "Boy?"

"Boy."

Her mom put a soft hand on hers and squeezed a little.

"Tell me."

Kassie was staring at her lap, examining her brown legs. So many people seemed to be so thrilled by them, and maybe she even liked to show them off sometimes just to see how guys would react, like with Maxim. But at this moment they seemed to be exactly only just what they were: legs. The attention they got tired her out.

She had an urge to tell her mom that she didn't want to talk. But she talked anyway.

"I really liked him," Kassie said.

"Who? That boy Connor?"

"Yes. But I started to think he was wrong for me."

"Why? Did he do something bad?"

This was the hard part. Kassie always avoided discussing this kind of thing with her mom, but her mood was so foul that she didn't care.

"Mom, it was like he was perfect. He would listen to me. We would have actual conversations and talk about real things, not just BS, you know what I mean? He wasn't just nodding his head to make me think he cared. All the things that I had built up in my head about who he was, from all those letters, he was the real thing. The real thing until I ... I got scared he'd turn out to be the kind of guy telling me that I need to stay home and not have a career, not go to college, just staying home and ... "

"And what?" her mom asked softly.

Kassie looked away. *Screw it*, she thought, *I'm saying it*.

"And doing nothing but raising kids and cooking and not being an engineer and not accomplishing anything at all."

It came out of her mouth harsh and bitter. She kept looking at the wall opposite where they sat. She didn't want to see her mom being hurt by her words. Her mom remained calm, silent, still. She was holding Kassie's hand.

Full of love, Kassie thought. *My mom is always so full of love.*

Kassie looked back and met her mother's gaze.

"I've been dreaming of being an engineer like Dad since I was a little girl, Mom. You know it. I was always watching him work, all the stuff he did for the space program. When we would spend some of our summers in Houston before we moved away from Hawaii, astronauts came to visit him at our house—and I spied on them!"

"Kassie, you're not supposed to spy!"

She eyed her mom silently for a moment.

"To be honest, I don't feel bad about it," Kassie said. "It was the most amazing thing ever, watching all of that go down. It got inside me. I knew I had the math whiz, from you and Aunt Brenda. The whole thing jelled for me. You and Dad encouraged me the whole way."

Kassie's mom kept smiling at her.

"I don't mean it's bad to raise kids, Mom. You're not less because—"

Her mom cut her off by laughing sweetly.

"Oh, Lord, honey," she said. "Nothing escapes you, but sometimes you don't see what you are even looking at. My feelings aren't hurt."

"No?"

"No, love," her mom said. "I was actually surprised—and maybe a little confused—at what you just told me."

"Why's that?"

"Your boy Connor," she said, squeezing Kassie's hand a little. "I had a chance to talk to him alone."

Kassie flushed.

"What did he say?"

"He told me an awful lot about how great you are, about how he wished he had the kind of ambition you do, that he wished he was anywhere near as talented and smart as you are. He said he'd love to do science one day, too, something about that science institute down there in Port Aransas. Dolphins, or something. Maybe sharks."

"The Marine Science Institute."

"Yeah, that. He said that before he met you he didn't know if he could do something like that, but that after meeting you he got inspired. He knew he could do it. He knew that you'd go to NASA one day and he would do marine biology."

Kassie was dumbfounded.

"You *will* do it," her mom said. "You will go and do those great things. Just because I decided not to doesn't mean you shouldn't."

"What? What do you mean?"

"I decided I wanted to be a stay-at-home mom. I wanted to do that. I could have been doing what Mary Jackson and Margaret Hamilton did. I had the gift, but that's not what I wanted—and it's OK. Just like it's OK if you don't become a stay-at-home mom when you're nineteen, like I did."

Kassie's hand reached for her throat, suddenly aware of a terrible pain there.

"Mom, I don't know what to say."

"Then don't say anything. Instead, go do something. Go do something about Connor."

THIRTY-ONE

DOWN IN THE GALLEY, Connor heard Stamford talking on the radio. There was some back and forth with the base station, then Stamford's head appeared as he leaned over from the bridge stairway. He peered down at Connor, grinning.

"We're going back home," Stamford said. "We need to pick up supplies and take them to a rig early tomorrow, so we gotta untie and head in. I'll back up close to the standpipe. You dive in and swim over, untie us, then jump aboard again. Easier this time, too, because you don't have to carry the rope!"

Connor went to the clear deck, balancing in a surfer pose as a joke, while Stamford backed the *Jayne Mansfield* toward the seaweed-draped and barnacle-encrusted leg of the standpipe. The stern hissed and splashed as it bounced into the oncoming swell.

Must be six feet, Connor thought.

Water blew out in every direction as the stern collided with the steep oncoming swell. The boat shuddered. For

Connor, it was unnerving watching waves two to three feet higher than the clear deck. Yet each time the stern rose above them. He moved close to the gunwale, ready for the plunge off the side. When the boat was about ten feet away Stamford put the boat in neutral and stuck his arm out the window, signaling him to go.

Connor dove in.

The cool dark-green water slapped him and enveloped his body in bubbles. He kicked firmly toward the nearest leg. Connor opened his eyes underwater. The standpipe's leg was a blurry vision, with fish cruising and scattering everywhere. The passing swells first impeded him, then propelled him forward. He surfaced, kicked and stroked his way to the ladder, made a grab for a rung—but the moss was too slick, and he slipped off. While he treaded water, another passing swell made him bang his knee on the barnacle- and oyster-covered leg, but it didn't hurt. The next time Connor tried to latch on his grip held fast. He clambered up. At the platform he clasped the railing at the gate, briefly glimpsing the stern of the boat rising up and down below. Stamford was maneuvering very close to the structure so Connor could jump down once he untied the rope. Connor had graduated from being scared to being wary. He swung himself up onto the grated steel platform. He looked down and noticed a trickle of blood running down his leg from the cut on his knee.

Battle scar, he thought. *Nothing to worry about.*

He untied the double half-hitch, coiled the slack as much as he could, and then heaved it hard toward the clear deck of the boat. It landed with a loud clop and unreeled into a tangled mess. Connor studied the rising and falling deck, judged the coming and going of the swell. Stamford held the boat in position, screws alternately still then violently tossing out bursts of foam. The rubber tire bumpers squeezed against the leg once, twice—and Connor leapt.

He landed just as the stern reached its peak.

Connor entered the crew cabin while *Jayne Mansfield* edged away from the rig.

When Stamford heard the cabin door bang closed he opened the throttles. A rooster tail shot out behind the boat and they were blasting their way back to Port Aransas. The sun was about an hour from setting, turning a deep yellow color against the bronzing sky.

On the bridge Stamford noticed blood on Connor's knee.

"Barnacles?" he asked.

"Yeah," Connor said.

"Damned things are big as your fist and sharp as razors. At least a sea urchin didn't get ya. Go down below and patch it up."

"In a bit," Connor answered, gazing out the bridge windows as the boat rose and fell in near-perfect timing with the following swell.

"What do you figure?" Connor asked, assessing the sea. "Six or eight?"

"Naw, maybe five at most," Stamford replied. "Weather says it'll be going flat tonight."

"Great. No waves again."

"Nope. Not that we'd have time to go out before duty calls anyway."

The boat came down hard on a swell; Connor and Stamford lurched forward. An explosion of whitewater blew up over the bow, then cascaded down over the bridge. The blast of spray didn't look like much, but it slapped the windows with a ferocious thump. Stamford turned a dial, and the wipers clunked back and forth.

"Damn," Connor muttered.

"Yeah," Stamford said. "I used to let that spray hit me when I was a deckhand. I'd pretend it was a barrel closing out on me. Kinda heavy sometimes."

"I still remember that barrel on Perfect Saturday ... "

"Aww, did you have to bring that up?" Stamford asked.

"That shocked look on your face was priceless," Connor said, smiling.

Stamford pulled a half-smoked joint out of a mashed pack of Marlboros that was on the dash, stuck it in his mouth and put a lighter to it. He took a deep hit, then offered it to Connor.

"Nah, I'm gonna have a beer instead."

"OK," Stamford said. "But first come over here and drive so I can finish this off."

Connor took the wheel and tried to keep the bow from plunging into the troughs, something that Stamford was so adept at. It was harder than he thought, but he did pretty well.

"Heard from Kassie?" Stamford asked nonchalantly.

"No. I'm pissed at her anyway. Hanging out with me the whole time she was here, and then on the last day, bam: She makes out with Maxim. What a bitch."

Stamford laughed at him.

"Made out with him?" Stamford said. "Are you shitting me? She rained all over his parade. I won me a hundred bucks off that wager."

Connor took his eyes off the sea and blinked at Stamford.

"What are you talking about?"

"Oh, hell. Didn't you know? I bet Maxim a hundred bucks that he wouldn't be able to get anywhere with Kassie. He's so full of himself that he took the bet. Sure enough, just like I said, he wasn't getting anywhere with her because—for some unknowable reason—she was hanging out with your lame ass the whole time."

Connor pretended to laugh as he kept his eyes on the swell.

"Well," he said, "I guess we did keep each other pretty busy."

"Damn you. Anyway, Maxim was running out of time, and he was really getting pissed because he didn't want to lose a hundred bucks. So when Kassie threw the party and invited everyone from the shop, he figured it was his last chance."

"Sandi knew about this?" Connor asked.

"Oh, yeah. You know that chick is some kind of sex freak. She wagered he wouldn't be able to score either. But then she egged him on even more by telling him she'd help out if he reeled the fish in."

Connor was dumbstruck but kept driving the *Jayne Mansfield* like it was the only thing on his mind. Stamford took another hit, the last of the joint, sucking so hard the tidbit roach held between his index finger and thumb flitted into his mouth. He burst out coughing and cursing.

"Damn it," he said, bending over and spitting. "I hate when that happens."

"You really should stick to Lone Star," Connor said. "So what happened after that?"

"Well, Maxim thought Kassie was flirting with him from the pool, challenging him to get into the water with her. So he stripped down to his board shorts, got in, and swam over. She was backing up, looking like she wanted to get away. Next thing I know he's making muscles for her. She was like totally making fun of him—'*Oh, wow, what big muscles you've got*'— that kinda thing. But he didn't even pick up on it. Instead, he traps her against the pool wall with his arms on both sides of her, and all of the sudden she tells him to back the fuck off. Then she went and kicked him! Then she jumped out of the water and left."

Connor said nothing.

"Man, you shoulda seen the look on Maxim's face," Stamford said. "Sandi nearly busted her gut laughing at him. Total fail. Kassie wasn't having any of his bullshit. And now I have a hundred-dollar bill in my pocket."

"Hey, man," Connor said, "I gotta go take a piss. Then I'm gonna clean the galley and crash for a bit."

"Yeah?" Stamford said. "Well, put some hydrogen peroxide on that scraped knee. I don't want you attracting sharks next time you have to tie us up to a rig."

THIRTY-TWO

KASSIE PICKED up the receiver from the hall phone and dialed Becky's number.

"Hello?"

"Hey, it's me."

"What's up, Kass?"

"I'm an idiot."

Becky laughed.

"What are you talking about?"

"I think I might have ruined it with him."

"I didn't think you'd use the word 'ruined' to describe what happened."

"Huh?" said Kassie, getting confused.

"Why do you think you're an idiot? We all agreed you should break up with Andrew."

Kassie slapped her forehead.

"Oh my God," she cried. "I'm not talking about Andrew. I'm talking about the guy from Port A. Remember I told you how upset I was with Connor for thinking I was cheating on him?"

"Oh, yeah. I wasn't sure. You were raving about him to us all. He sounded good—definitely looked good. I think you said he reminded you of your Uncle Alan. You said he was the jealous type. I didn't get that impression, but I know how you feel about jealousy. So ... second thoughts?"

"I'm in love with him."

Becky paused.

"So then he *doesn't* remind you of your Uncle Alan?"

"I don't know, Becky. I need your help. All the things I told you about him at first are the true things. I just blew it. I provoked Maxim when I got drunk."

"Well, I wanted to provoke Maxim too. Heck, all of us wanted to provoke him. Alex was crazy about him, but in the end she settled for Kevin."

"Blech," Kassie said. "She can have both. Here's the thing. I need you to tell me what you'd do if you were in love with someone but fucked it up and needed to apologize—but at the same time you needed to admit that they were right and you actually had been flirting with someone else."

"Don't tell him that."

"I have to. Otherwise he won't trust me."

"Do you want my advice or not?" asked Becky, laughing. She felt bad for her friend, but also felt that Kassie telling Connor that she'd been trying to provoke Maxim when he had his back turned wouldn't go well.

"Listen," Kassie said. "It's way deeper than I told you before."

"Tell me."

Kassie told her everything, including what had happened at the beach when they'd lost control of themselves. It was hard, because Becky went to the same church, and Kassie was afraid she might tell her to confess all of her illicit activity.

But Becky didn't do that. She listened very quietly to Kassie's story.

"Well," Kassie asked after divulging every detail, "what do I do now?"

"Wow, Kassie," Becky said. "Knowing you so well, and having watched some of this unfold, I think you can have both."

"What? That's crazy. I can't have Maxim and Connor. I don't even want that!"

Becky burst out laughing, couldn't seem to stop, and Kassie started to get her feelings hurt.

"Hey," she protested, "I didn't call you to make me feel worse!"

"I'm sorry, Kass," Becky said, collecting herself. "I didn't expect you to say that. I meant that you can have both aerospace engineering and Connor. He's nothing like your Uncle Alan. Maybe in the long run the big challenge will be the whole God and church thing. But for now it's really very simple."

Becky was alluding to the fact that Connor did not go to church and had told Kassie he was on the agnostic side. Becky waited until Kassie prompted her to continue.

"Well come on," Kassie said, impatient to hear Becky's solution. "What's so simple about this?"

"What big message do we hear all the time from the church? No sex until marriage, no birth control—even condoms are banned. Isn't that part of your problem? Isn't the possibility of having children and having to drop out of school before you get your degree the biggest thing scaring you away from Connor?"

"He's the jealous type ... " Kassie started to say.

"No, Kass. You know in your heart he's not. The thing with Maxim, you can explain that and he'll understand. I'm telling you to go get Connor. You have to make a break with what we've been told since we were little girls. You just need to protect yourself against an unplanned pregnancy."

"Mom would die if I were having unmarried sex."

"I've kept something from you," Becky said. "But if you promise not to tell anyone else, I'll tell you a secret. It's critical, Kass—absolutely critical—that you never tell anyone."

Kassie was silent for a moment. She sensed a growing chagrin, maybe even a bit of hurt that Becky felt the need to prompt her for secrecy. They had been best friends since Kassie had moved to Midland and met her at church.

"Your secret is good with me," Kassie said. "I'll never tell a soul."

"I'm on the pill," Becky said.

THIRTY-THREE

"DAMN," Connor said to himself. "I'm a complete dipshit."

He was holding onto the galley table as the boat jumped from the top of one swell to the next. Connor couldn't see anything below deck, but after one week of work on the boat he'd gotten used to how it moved. Now, the bumping and jarring hardly bothered him at all. But what did bother him was the revelation that he'd jumped to conclusions about what Kassie had been doing in the pool when Maxim cornered her.

He snatched a cold Lone Star from the fridge, cracked it open, and slammed some down. Then, for good measure, he slugged more and more until an ice cream headache seemed to crack his skull, like it had been hit with a steel wedge.

He stopped, winced, but the pain didn't make the sorrow about Kassie dissipate.

She had tried to tell him what had happened.

Despondent, he climbed the narrow stairway up to the crew cabin and lurched from one table to the next, grabbing the tables as he went with his free hand, holding his beer in the other. At the door, he held onto the handle as he watched the wake, the narrow whitewater wash from the spinning props in the center, the wedge of foam left behind in the swell. He saw the occasional plume of spray wash back from the bow. It splashed in a thin sheet, like rain, over the clear deck and stern.

"That looks like fun," he said.

He opened the hatch and stepped out. All he could hear was the engine noise, the slamming of the boat, and the rain of spray across the clear deck. Connor closed the hatch behind him and stood in the wind. The *Jayne Mansfield* was making a good twenty knots. Stamford didn't screw around when it came to getting back to harbor after work. Steak and potatoes were on the menu tonight—ice cream, too—and then a good joint and bed. Connor would meet the delivery truck and bring the food on board while Stamford was in dreamland.

Connor remembered the surfing game Stamford used to play as he downed the rest of his Lone Star, crushed the can in his fist, then threw it hard upward. It only went up about three feet before the wind snatched it. The can went sailing over the stern, gone in an instant.

Gone. Just like Kassie, he thought, *or his Mom.*

On a lark he crouched down on all fours and moved down toward the middle of the clear deck, balancing against the pitching of the deck, which seemed to follow a pretty steady rhythm. Then, like he was catching a wave, he suddenly snapped up, standing in a fake crouched surf pose like he was looking down a perfectly wedge-shaped line.

The boat heaved up so suddenly that when it fell back down Connor was lifted up off the deck, feeling weightless. There was a huge impact as the boat plowed hard into the swell. Connor couldn't see the solid sheet of whitewater rise on both sides of the bow. He had been knocked off balance by the impact and was trying to get his footing when he spun around toward the bow.

A thick wall of whitewater hit him in the face and chest.

Connor tumbled backward over the clear deck, the ropes, a coiled hose, laughing because it felt like being pummeled by a big wave after wiping out. He was dragged along, surrounded by a foamy fizz of water and bubbles under the sea. And then his head burst up out of the water in the middle of *Jayne Mansfield's* wake.

The gray and white boat plowed on.

Connor laughed out loud.

"Oh, shit."

He wasn't yelling after what had happened, because he knew Stamford would swing around any second to pull alongside, call him an idiot, and then throw him one of the orange life rings with *Jayne Mansfield* painted in coarse black letters.

But the boat kept right on going, getting smaller and smaller in the distance as the swell lifted him up, then down. Soon he could only see the boat when the swell lifted him up high, and then he couldn't see it at all. And, still waiting, he found himself only able to hear the boat's distant drone. A few moments later all he heard was the water rising and falling and the occasional slosh of a cresting wave.

It was the slow, indifferent song of the deep.

THIRTY-FOUR

STAMFORD REALLY LOVED CAPTAINING the crew boat. He'd liked fishing boat work, but this was way better. First off, crew boats had more power and were bigger and therefore more rewarding to pilot. He thought of his first experience with Uncle Jack's forty-five-foot Hatteras. Uncle Jack—"Unck" for short—would let him man the bridge while Ben and Robinson were fishing. Unck would smoke cigars and drink whiskey sours, and Stamford had learned how to drive that Hatteras like an expert. No tight maneuver seemed beyond his abilities. But the *Jayne Mansfield* was a whole different beast.

The Hatteras also served as a party boat that girls totally dug and went crazy on. He could remember weekend after weekend of bringing girls back to Unck's place and taking them onto the Hatteras, where beer was in the fridge, reefer in the cupboard, and tequila in the freezer.

"Tequila shots," Stamford said to himself, laughing: They were the only reliable wingmen he'd ever known.

As the *Jayne Mansfield* came around the end of the south

jetty he looked and saw the swell breaking on its end, remembered the time he'd taken Julie Southfield out there in the middle of the night and they'd gotten it on right on a big block of granite, nothing but the sound of the small black swell washing gently on the rock and the moonlit sky above. There had been no breeze to mask their whispers, moans, and finally Stamford's loud voice, saying, "I'm coming." After he'd said that, a gruff old man's voice not far off replied: "That's great, kid. Now get the hell out of here. You're scaring the fish away."

Stamford chuckled at the memory. Julie had yanked her clothes back on, and they'd indeed gotten the hell out of there. They'd laughed all the way back to her house, where they did it again in the front seat of his truck.

In the ship channel Stamford slowed the diesels down to about fifty percent power. The boat settled into a deeper posture in the water and the wake got heavier.

Looking behind him, Stamford thought about how he and Connor needed to do some wake surfing behind the boat.

"Hey, Connor!" Stamford shouted down the stairwell to the galley. "We're about five minutes out from the harbor. Better get out of bed you lazy ass."

Connor didn't answer, but that didn't strike Stamford as unusual. He figured Connor was asleep. He also wasn't on the clear deck making ready for when they pulled up to the dock, but there was plenty of time. They weren't even to the harbor yet.

The *Jayne Mansfield* hummed right past the Marine Science Institute on the south side and the Jetty Boat dock on the north side. Ferry boats transiting the channel hove into view.

There were no freighters or tankers, no barges or shrimp

boats, no deep sea or other fishing boats to be concerned about. He had the channel to himself.

A minute later the boat transited across the intersection of the Intracoastal Waterway and Corpus Christi ship channel. Stamford saw a sailboat plying the Lydia Ann Channel, then glimpsed the distant lighthouse. The sun, now just fifteen minutes above the horizon, made him squint, and he saw some cumulus building out west. The water was a dark green, smoothing with the dying wind. Stamford slowed the boat to a crawl and maneuvered between the Port Aransas Harbor entrance jetties.

He checked the clear deck and was immediately annoyed that Connor wasn't there. He darted back to the stairway and yelled down into the galley: "Hey get out on deck, man! You gotta tie us up!"

The *Jayne Mansfield* was in the glassy water of the harbor. It slid past the Wharf Cat and Scat Cat charter boats that Stamford had worked on one summer. That had been awesome, right up until it wasn't. The tourists would drop in their lines with electric reels on short rods sticking out just two feet over the sides, locked in small tubes to keep them from falling overboard. It was his job to put the rods out, bait the hooks, gaff the fish the tourists pulled in. Half of them were vomiting over the sides before a single line dropped, and sharks circled the boat in droves. *God help them if the boat were to sink,* Stamford recalled thinking. There had been sixty people on board—and seven small life rafts between them.

Still no sign of Connor.

Stamford was getting pissed, but he focused on pulling the boat in exactly, and in fact, he brought it in within a half a foot of the floating dock, stopped a good ten feet from the cement harbor edge. He hopped down the stairs to the crew cabin and ran down toward the hatch cursing Connor as loud has he could.

"Goddamn! I oughta fire your ass for this bullshit!" he yelled.

Out on deck he grabbed the stern tie-up rope and got it secured to the dock cleat, then ran up to the front; he threw the front line onto the dock, jumped over the side, twisting his slap sideways and pinching his toe.

"Damn it," he said, wincing, as he secured the boat. "There will be words, Connor O'Reilly. There are definitely going to be words."

Good thing a west wind wasn't blowing, he thought.

Stamford walked briskly back to the clear deck. He hopped on board, then marched angrily to the crew cabin hatch and jerked it open, letting it slam behind him as he strode inside.

"Connor fuckin' O'Reilly, I am going to kick your fucking ass, man!"

Stamford descended into the galley and jerked open the curtain to the bunks, fully expecting to find Connor snoring away.

But he wasn't there.

"What the hell?" Stamford said. He turned and pounded on the head door.

"Hey!" he yelled. "Are you fucking dead or something in there?"

Reaching down he saw that the little indicator on the doorknob said "unoccupied" so he twisted the knob and pulled it open an inch or two, just in case Connor was pinching a loaf, which might at least be excusable.

It, too, was empty.

Stamford stepped back, suddenly not feeling very good. A pang of fear shot through him.

"Connor!" he yelled. "Connor! Are you fucking with me, Connor? You'd better be fucking with me, man!"

Stamford ran through the boat, checking everywhere, talking to himself the whole time, begging Connor to stop fucking with him, to come out from where he was hiding. He even checked under the bench seats to see if he'd find his deckhand cracking up when he lifted the lid.

Finally he went onto the clear deck fully expecting Connor to jump out from the other side of the main cabin, laughing his ass off. It was then that he saw one of Connor's flip-flops wedged between the deck and the stern's six-inch-high gunwale.

THIRTY-FIVE

WEAR LONG PANTS, Connor thought to himself. *Next time, wear long pants.*

In his mind he was picturing how as kids at the Young Life pool they'd had a demonstration of how to use their jeans as a life preserver. The instructor was standing in the pool in jeans and a T-shirt, explaining how to do it, then he moved to the deep end for a demonstration.

Connor and the rest of the kids had laughed as the guy made a joke out of getting out of his jeans in the water. "Don't worry," he'd said. "I'm not wearing any underwear!"

It looked like an ordeal, tying knots in the legs and filling the wet jeans with air by swooping them overhead, but it eventually worked. The trainer had been exhausted by the effort, breathing hard.

"You have to refill with air every once in a while," he'd said, "but it will keep you above water until help comes."

Right, Connor thought.

He was treading water in his surf baggies and T-shirt. Then, without even thinking about it, he rolled over onto his back and started slowly back stroking toward the west—toward shore, where the sun was going down.

Treading water would exhaust him in less than an hour. He figured the rescuers would find him by then, but he didn't want to take any chances in case they didn't. The Gulf swell was moving east to west, pushing him toward shore, so at least he had that going for him. He remembered the weather radio saying the swell would transition to calm seas at night.

It was creepy in the dark-green water, the sky paling above. He tried to swim smoothly and without splashing. To calm his pounding heart he pretended that Stamford had probably noticed he was overboard. About ten minutes had gone by since he'd last heard the *Jayne Mansfield*'s big diesels and he figured to hear them again any second.

But every time Connor was sure he heard the sound of approaching crew boat and snapped up in the water, treading and kicking hard to lift himself up as far as possible on the swell peaks, he saw and heard nothing.

At some point he realized he'd completely lost track of how long he'd been in the water. Had it been thirty minutes, like it felt, or just five? Had it been an hour? The sun informed him that time was running out, however long he'd been in the drink.

"Fine," Connor said out loud. "Stamford, you son of a bitch, when I get to the beach I'm gonna walk all the way to the harbor and punch your ass right in the face."

Connor found that periodically cursing his friend helped calm him down. He was feeling strong and knew that with the swell direction and his backstroking he was only a couple of hours from shore. He was sure he could do it.

"I ain't going down this way," he said to the Gulf and the sky. "Not this way, not this day."

A stray cross-chop bumped into a swell that he was rising

up with and a small wave broke across his face, pushing water into his nose and making him sputter and spit. The saltwater burned his eyes. But it also reminded him of wiping out while surfing.

"That swell will become a wave soon," he said. "It'll be a good wave. Somebody will see it at the third bar by the pier. They'll paddle toward it, they'll catch it, and they'll get barreled."

Clint was shocked.

"So you're telling me you didn't notice Connor was overboard until you got to the dock?"

"He always stays below deck on the way in." Stamford said, feeling humiliated. "I didn't even think about it."

"Have you told the Coast Guard?"

"I called them first. I told them the route we took on the way in, and they told me to stand by on emergency frequency."

"All right," Clint said. "Listen, it's at least an hour before dark. They'll find him. I'll be in contact with them, too, and I'll let you know when I hear the good news."

But when Clint and Stamford hung up, neither one of them was feeling very good. Clint had to call Connor's dad and tell him he'd fallen overboard and was lost at sea. Stamford was shaking like it was freezing cold. He went outside the tiny harbormaster's building and heard the search helicopter's turbines spooling up over at the Coast Guard station.

After a few moments, he heard the steady flap and chop of the blades spinning, they increased speed, and then the chopper climbed up into view and turned east to fly out over the jetty and search back along the *Jane Mansfield's* route.

"They'll be sending out cutters, too," Stamford said to himself.

He didn't go to church anymore, but as he hurried back to the bridge to monitor the radio he stumbled through a silent prayer.

If they don't find him alive, he thought, gazing at the harbor, *I'm done.*

THIRTY-SIX

KASSIE HAD RUN the conversation through in her head a million times during the day. She tried to imagine every variation of what might happen and how she could try to get back to where they had been before the party.

She figured Connor wouldn't be home until evening. At dinner she shoveled her food down so fast that she was finished before the rest of her family were even halfway done.

"Can I be excused, please?"

Her dad looked surprised, but her mom understood Kassie's haste and gave her permission.

"Sure honey, go ahead," her mom said as she looked at Kassie's dad in a way that told him not to ask.

Kassie took her empty plate and silverware to the kitchen, then went to the hall phone. She picked up the receiver, put it back, picked it up again, then put it back on the cradle. She eventually got as far as pushing the buttons, but clapped the receiver back down before the connection was made. She felt butterflies in her stomach.

What she wanted was to go back in time and erase the

way she'd acted at the party. She'd been pretty drunk, she admitted to herself, so it wasn't just Connor being a dumbass. She'd been an idiot to provoke Maxim. It had been an impulse she knew in her gut was wrong to follow, but the tequila had clouded her judgment and Maxim had reacted exactly as she should have expected.

She felt a powerful need to tell Connor the truth, that she had given in to a flirtatious whim. It was the truth, after all. But she wasn't going to start with that story, because it might make things worse.

The plan was to tell Connor that he was the only guy she was interested in. She wanted him to come out to Cali and be with her while she went to school. She wanted someone who cared about all the things she did—someone who could understand how hard the thing was that she was about to undertake. Later, after things were patched up, she would confess anything else that needed to be cleared up. But not until things were certain.

Kassie raised her eyebrows at her rationalizing.

Bullshit, she told herself. *You want Connor because you're in love with him. Now get on with it.*

There was the phone, waiting.

She dialed his number. Her throat felt so tight that she thought she might squeak instead of talk when he answered. The phone kept ringing, though, with no answer, and Kassie started to feel weird. She hadn't imagined no one answering. She started to lower the receiver back to the cradle in disappointment when she heard a man answer.

"Hello?"

She snatched the phone back to her head, spoke so quickly that her words were mashed together: "Hi-it's-Kassie-is-Connor-around?"

There was a pause.

"Sorry, what was that?"

Kassie took a breath.

"It's Kassie. Connor and I hung out this summer, and I wanted to talk with him."

There was silence on the other end.

"Hello?" she said. "Are you there?"

"Yeah, yeah, I'm here," said the man, sounding confused. "Who are you again?"

This was not going as expected. Kassie began to wonder if she had dialed the wrong number.

"I'm ... well, I'm Connor's friend Kassie. We were ... well, we spent some time together this last summer, and I ... "

"Oh, yes. Kassie. I remember. Yeah, I'm Connor's dad. Yeah ... he, uh ... he really liked you."

Kassie wasn't prepared to hear the past tense used to refer to Connor.

"I mean, I just wanted to say hi really quick if he's there," she said.

More silence on the line.

"I'm his dad," the man repeated, softly. Kassie's fear of being rejected started to morph into a tangled knot in her belly. She just knew that he was about to tell her that Connor didn't want to talk to her—that he wouldn't speak to her and didn't want to hear from her again.

"I'm sorry, Kassie," Connor's dad continued. "I have some tough news."

Kassie felt her heart drop.

It was true, she thought. *She'd ruined everything, and it was over.*

Connor's dad hesitated, then: "It's not been a good day. Connor is missing."

Kassie was completely dumbfounded.

"What? I'm sorry. I don't understand. Missing?"

Connor's dad cleared his throat.

"Missing. Yeah, that's the word they used. He fell off the crew boat when it was coming in from a rig. They called me, they said he was missing. They haven't found him. He's lost at sea."

Stars—

Look at those stars, Connor thought. He'd never seen such nighttime stars. A black space painted by brilliant pinpoints and faint smears of nebulae stretching from one side of the wide horizon to the other, all the way around, no matter which way he turned. Amazing—and beautiful.

It was also amazing he still didn't feel tired. He should be tired, but the elementary backstroke had never seemed to tire him—and now it was saving his life.

"I will not be tired," he said to the stars.

My life depends on it.

His life, which had collapsed to this moment—and what would soon come of it.

Connor drummed up all kinds of thoughts to keep his mind off where he was and what he was doing. He remembered when he first started surfing, back when he and his friends would see some of the older surfers or the ones who were only pretend surfers smoking weed under the pier. Connor admired the older surfers; they could paddle toward an incoming wave, spin at the last second, stroke once and then drop in on an overhead wave already starting to break. They would slash a tremendous bottom turn and fly straight back up the face for a vertical off-the-lip. But he had nothing but contempt for the pretend surfers. Sometimes the phonies paddled out, but they had no stamina because their lungs were wasted from smoking, and their muscles were weak. They floundered and got washed in with the big sets or their boards would be torn away from them to go spinning through the air and smack loudly on the barnacle-encrusted black pilings of the pier.

Other times Connor and his friends would sit in their cars and read *Surfer* and *Surfing* magazines, wishing that their waves were as big and hollow as the waves in Hawaii, but their waves were rarely hollow like those on the North Shore. Their water wasn't blue, but green or brown instead. In December blooms of cabbagehead jellyfish would fill the water. The cabbagehead made great weapons. Someone would grab one and throw it at somebody else. It would arc through the air, unseen by the victim, water spinning off, until—SPLOTCH—it hit. That guy would get pissed and soon the cabbageheads would be flying around to hoots and hollers—and a lot of splotch sounds and curses.

Mostly they didn't hurt, but you never knew; cabbageheads with dark feathering at the edge would sometimes sting badly. If one of those hit you in the face, you were fucked.

Only one guy ever got hit in the face. "My eyes! My eyes!" he yelled and paddled in. But no one paid attention because he was from Corpus.

Connor laughed at the black sky and the stars.

"Now who's fucked?" he yelled—and the only answer was a slosh of water from a swell he couldn't see.

THIRTY-SEVEN

KASSIE WAS DOING SEVENTY-FIVE, top down. The Corvair hummed, its gas pedal close to the floorboard. The balmy night air kept her comfortable and the air-cooled, six-cylinder Corvair motor loved it, too. She watched the additional gauges her dad had put in to keep track of the engine: oil temp 190 degrees, head temp 345 degrees—pretty much perfect, and way below having to worry about it. These cars could run forever if well-maintained.

Good God, she thought. *I'm such a fucking nerd.*

It was embarrassing, so she hid her geekiness from most people. She only cut loose around her family—and Connor.

Even at twenty miles an hour over the double-nickel speed limit, it was going to take eight hours to get to Port A. On the dash, her dad's Fuzzbuster II glowed amber. The light pulsed dimly, but if a radar gun was aimed in her direction it would brighten and squeal.

But she didn't care how many tickets she got.

The pressure she felt inside her body, the raw tension of fearing for Connor's life, was making her feel nauseous.

Having the top down kept her focused on what mattered most: reeling in the miles until there were none between her and Connor O'Reilly.

Luckily, Interstate 10 had huge stretches with hardly any other traffic.

The sky above her was brilliant with fall constellations—no moon—and she thought of the Gulf at night: vast, black, indifferent. She could look up and see the Milky Way where she was, and maybe it was what Connor was seeing. The Big Dipper, the Little Dipper, Polaris—it had to be what he was seeing. The same bright stars, Jupiter overhead, Saturn just coming over the horizon. She threw prayers at the planets and the sky but focused on the long, straight road ahead.

"Please, God," she pleaded. "Please don't let him die."

Maybe by his determination and by the strength he had built up from all the years of surfing, and with God's grace, he could hold out until the Coast Guard found him. She would confess everything, and especially the incident with Maxim. Most of all—most important of all—he had to be told what she'd been planning to say to him after the party, when she had him finally to herself.

Connor felt the first hint of being tired.

No, he thought. *I cannot let fatigue set in already.*

He decided to ease up on how fast he was doing his backstroke and instead concentrate on wasting no movement. He refocused his mind and sought out Polaris in the night sky. He could see the Big Dipper, bright and unmistakable, and his eyes traced along the bottom of the cup out to the North Star.

There!

It was instant relief. He'd never felt so bizarrely lost, with nothing around him but that one point of light to let him know where he was. Even the faint glow to the west had faded to black.

He had to keep Polaris on his left, ninety degrees to port.

Elementary backstroke to the west, Connor thought. *Keep heading west. Easy does it. Steady.*

The water seemed to go on forever on either side of him, black and calmly rising and falling, faint sounds of nearer and farther splashes of water that merged mercilessly into the black of the night sky but for the stars, the Milky Way. Such a vision of it he'd never seen, in a circumstance he never would have sought.

If these really were the last of the days and nights of his life, he wondered, what part of it would he want to have of its short duration—to feel again, to live through again, just once more? Of all those pretty stars, how many had planets where there was strife and war, sadness and depression, love and loss? How many screaming matches were happening right now? How many of those who lived on those planets were in the throes of passion or of regret—and how many were swimming for their very lives?

For Connor, it wasn't even Kassie's face, the lithe curve of her taut belly when she leaned back and laughed, or the way her eyes flashed with joy. All those things were great, but what he remembered was the power of her wrapped around him under the dark night sky, when they parked on the beach after *Free Ride*. He thought of her lips meeting his and pressing themselves into each other. Of all the things that mattered in his life it was being with her, around her, in her, that filled his mind. That shining moment on the beach, with these stars that her own eyes had seen when she lay under him, running her hands through his hair—pulled him in, and then that moment when the stars were outshone by the bright white of a Coast Guard helicopter's searchlight.

Connor slowly realized he was hearing the distant sound of a helicopter. Somebody was looking for him.

Ripped out of his reverie he spun upright and began treading water, slowly so as to conserve energy, turning with each swell's rise. Then he saw it: a Coast Guard chopper's searchlight slicing back and forth across the black water.

Far out to sea.

"Shit," Connor blurted out loud.

Disoriented and in a wild tumult of hope, he started shouting, waving, cursing: "Over here! Over here!"

He kept lurching up, waving, yelling, hoping.

Then he stopped cold, realizing there wasn't a chance in hell they could see him. He watched for a few minutes as the chopper moved further and further away.

I'm fucked, he thought, and he really believed it.

He lay back down in the water and resumed his backstroke, keeping his eyes on Polaris.

Clint, on the phone with Connor's dad again, told him the Coast Guard had given up about an hour after dark; the crews would resume the search one hour before civil twilight the next morning.

"What does that mean?" Connor's dad asked.

"About an hour before the sky starts getting light," Clint replied. "I'm ... Mr. O'Reilly, I believe that your son is alive and that we will find him and bring him home."

"I want to think so too, Clint."

"Good night, Mr. O'Reilly."

"Good night."

Clint hung up and looked at Stamford.

"So you said you charted the area he might be in?" he asked.

After Stamford had alerted the Coast Guard, he'd listened to the marine weather broadcast. There was a southeast wind at less than five knots, a southeasterly current at three knots, and swell southeast at three, with calm seas by morning.

He'd spread a chart out on a table, had drawn a line between the standpipe where they'd been and the south jetty. Then he'd drawn an X on the spot he figured the *Jayne Mansfield* was when Connor said he was going below. He put another X on the line a mile from the end of the south jetty, and with a plotter he drew lines from each X to the beach, angling the same direction as the wind and the current.

Stamford showed the search area he'd drawn to Clint.

"He's somewhere in there," Stamford said. "I gave the coordinates of the limits of the search area to the Coast Guard. They're using it."

"All right," Clint said. "I'm going back to the police station. I wish I could understand how this happened. I don't want you getting into trouble, or any kind of investigation happening. Make sure your boat is clean. Get my meaning?"

"Dude, I didn't shove him over the side, for fuck's sake!" Stamford said, grabbing both sides of his head with his hands and looking at the chart on the table.

To Clint it looked like Stamford was about to cry—but he didn't. Instead, he looked up and said, "We've been friends for years. I'm going to find him, or the Coast Guard or one of the boats in this harbor will."

Clint pressed his lips together.

"It ain't your fault, Kevin," he said. "Just make sure your

boat is absolutely squeaky clean. Like, go after any residue with a lot of soap, and then Clorox, OK?"

Stamford stared at the floor.

"It's clean, man. I can guarantee that."

"Good," Clint answered. "I'm outta here.

Clint stood.

"I'll let you know any more details about the search frequencies and so on tomorrow."

"Right," Stamford said.

Clint left the harbormaster's office, got in his squad car, and drove off.

It was quiet except for the boat's generator hum.

Stamford knew he'd be leaving harbor with the *Jayne Mansfield* and be out the jetties at first light. He'd given the coordinates to the Coast Guard, then called everyone he knew with a fishing boat and told them what happened, passing along the coordinates of the search area as he did so.

He had surf shop employees set up as volunteers to be lookouts. The owners of the small fleet of fishing boats began prepping to go out, and the workers at Woody's Boat Basin were filling up gas tanks in the middle of the night. Everyone in town who could was planning to head out near dawn and start looking. There was no way they were going to let Connor O'Reilly go down without an all-hands-on-deck effort.

After Clint left, Stamford needed to double-check that there was nothing incriminating on the boat. But he was so overwrought and wasted by nervous exertion and concern that he had to lie down. He went to the bridge and turned the radio up, just in case, then went below to his bunk.

At first, he remembered all the great things he and Connor had done together. There was the time they'd gotten completely wasted and grabbed leftover iron plumbing pipes

—and a load of fireworks left over from New Year's—and had driven in a convoy with Franklin, Robinson, Castle, and Cal Steiner way down the island. They had gone into the dunes and shot bottle rockets and Roman candles at each other. Half of the fireworks had failed, rooster tails of sparks flashing briefly as one volley missed after the next, until Steiner got hit square in the chest by a fireball that exploded when it hit him. It had caught his shirt on fire, searing his skin.

Everyone had laughed as Steiner struggled to remove his flaming shirt.

"Damn it, Robinson!" he had yelled. "I'm gonna kick your ass!"

Steiner had grabbed an iron pipe and chased Robinson off into the dunes, shouting: "Come out, come out, wherever you are!"

But Robinson had said nothing. He wouldn't come back, even after Steiner had promised not to bust him over the head with the pipe or hurt him in any way.

"You ruined my shirt, man!" Steiner had shouted into the dark.

They'd been so drunk that they wandered back to their cars and drove home.

They saw Robinson the next day at school, grinning from ear to ear.

"Eh," he said, "I oughta kick all y'all's asses!"

And then there was the time Franklin, in his white postal jeep, went careening through Charlie's Pasture at 3 a.m., drunk, high, rampaging—suddenly the jeep went up on two wheels. Stamford and Connor were bouncing around in the back, shouting and screaming like crazed apes in a cage.

There also was the time he and Connor had been sitting in front of the Rock Cottages with Saunders in junior high when their good friend, teetotaler Keith Ellison, drove by in his blue station wagon. There were a bunch of college girls in it. They started yelling "stop, stop!" Ellison hit the brakes, whipped a U-turn and came back to get the boys. They piled into the back of his station wagon—but after twenty minutes of driving around, with the girls telling them how horny they were and how they wanted to get laid, Connor had said, "I need to go home or I'll get in trouble with my dad."

"I can't believe it, Connor," Stamford said aloud. "First you ruin us getting laid—and now, damn it, you're ruining my career as a crew boat captain."

THIRTY-EIGHT

IT HAD TO END SOON.

The sky faded in and out and the slosh of the water at first seemed far away, then it gurgled like a draining bathtub. His mom was leaning over him with a towel: "Time to get out, honey."

Something bumped his leg.

Fear pulsed through Connor's body. A moment later, again, something big bumped his leg. Connor closed his eyes and remained perfectly still.

Shark.

So this is how it ends, Connor thought. *I won't be studying marine biology. Marine biology will be studying me.*

"Honey," he heard his mom say, "it'll be OK. You'll be OK."

"Where are you, Mom?"

"Right here."

"So am I," his dad added. "We're both here."

But when Connor opened his eyes, he saw only the starry sky above. No sign of his mom or dad.

"Listen, buddy," he heard his dad say, in that way he talked when he was about to deliver some hard-won wisdom. "I know you like that girl Kassie. I know you think maybe she was not being true with you, but I think you're wrong. You didn't even try to talk to her at the party after you got mad. You just walked off. But here's the thing: She came after you, didn't she?"

Connor saw a meteor streak across the Milky Way. It was big, fat, and flared into a bright fireball trailing a smoke trail. Then it was gone.

"I know," he said softly to his dad. "I blew it over a hundred-dollar bet."

The water swished violently nearby.

"You know what to do now, don't you?" his dad asked.

When Connor replied, it seemed like he was speaking from outside his own body, even though he was still inside his own head: "I'm not going to make it, Dad."

"Like hell," his dad said. "You *are* going to make it. You are *not* going to give up. You've got way too many things left to do."

"You can pull through, honey," his mom added. "I'm here for you."

At first, Connor was crying, then he wasn't. Then he was waiting. He had no more strength left to swim. Every muscle was defeated, every fiber of his mind exhausted. Any moment now, his body, turned belly up to stay afloat, would be shredded by a beast ten times his size. It had dead, black eyes, and a sense of smell so keen that it could detect every molecule of fear oozing from his body. Why wouldn't the damn thing strike? Connor felt the raw cruelty of knowing a horrible death was just a few short seconds away.

But nothing happened.

Then it was much later and he woke up and it was dawn.

He heard a loud splash of water in the calm sea and figured it had to be the shark coming for him, a last sudden thrust, in for the kill—

The wind suddenly whipped up and rain stormed heavily over him, filled his nostrils and mouth. To Connor, it was a perfect end. All he needed to do was sink into the salty serenity of the deep and let the lightning-quick shark attack take him out.

A shadow crossed the gray dawn sky.

Connor heard another loud splash. Cursing, he yelled: "Stop tormenting me!"

His back muscles finally gave out. Connor flattened, he sank below the surface.

I actually do love her. It was a fine last thought. He held it close.

Then Connor was grabbed from below and shoved up hard. His eyes blinked open, realizing his body had been yanked up out of the water.

No blood.

"Got you," he heard a strong voice say.

It was a man, arms reaching from behind, and then another man appeared in front of him, wearing a face mask and a wetsuit.

"We got you, Connor!"

The men wrapped an orange rescue loop under both his arms and cinched it behind his lolling head. One of them looked up at the chopper, then raised his arm and swirled it. The winch started to haul Connor up; he swayed wildly and saw the Gulf recede below him. The twisting cable spun him as he rose, and he saw three bottlenose dolphins circling around the divers.

Strong hands pulled him into the warm cabin of the helicopter.

He began shivering uncontrollably, muttering about the dolphins, reaching out with his hands, but the rescuers pushed his arms down and wrapped him with blankets and asked him to be still. He saw their mouths moving as they spoke into headsets, but he couldn't hear anything over the engine whine and the thumping of the rotors. A warm hand rested on his head, a face leaned over and smiled.

Coast Guard, Connor thought, and faded.

THIRTY-NINE

"WE GOT HIM!" Clint said into the phone. "He's alive all right. He's alive, and they're flying him straight over to Spohn Hospital in Corpus."

"Oh my dear Lord," Connor's father answered. His heart filled with joy and his eyes welled up with tears.

The next to get notified was Stamford.

"You're off the hook, my friend," Clint told him, over the marine radio. "Coast Guard picked him up at six this morning. They used your map, bro!"

Relief flooded Stamford's whole body.

After that, Clint had driven over to Gulf Beach Cottages in a police car so he could give Steve O'Reilly a high-speed escort down the Island Road. Clint kept his lights on the whole time until they turned into the parking lot at Spohn.

The doctor on duty talked to Connor's dad at the floor station.

"The kid has some strength to stay afloat all night in the Gulf," the doctor said. "He was seriously dehydrated and exhausted, and he had some hypothermia. But he'll be fine."

The charge nurse led Steve O'Reilly to his son's room.

When his dad walked in, Connor looked over at him and grinned.

"Don't worry," he said. "I'm about to call Stamford and quit."

Connor's dad walked over and grabbed him, hugging him so hard that Connor's eyes bulged.

"Whoa, there," he said.

"I thought I'd lost you," his dad said, voice cracking.

It sounded to Connor like his dad was crying. He wrapped his arms around his dad's back, felt his dad's whiskers against his neck and cheek. Three hours before, he'd made peace with never embracing his father again.

"Hey, at least you could've shaved before showing up," Connor joked.

"Thank God you're safe," he heard his dad answer.

Connor's dad stopped hugging him and stood up. Still pressed against the hospital bed, he looked at Connor square on, then clasped one of his hands.

"What the hell happened?" he asked.

Connor was embarrassed, but he explained without hiding what an idiot he'd been.

"So, Dad, you can see it really wasn't Stamford's fault."

"Even so, I'm not happy with him."

"Well, me neither, but I'm the one who told him I was going below to crash out," Connor said. "I did that all the time. I'd go below to get things cleaned up, or I'd take a nap on the way in. He said he'd call me when we got to the harbor breakwater. That's probably when he figured out I was missing."

His dad frowned, folded his arms over his chest.

"I'd honestly prefer to be pissed off at Stamford."

"Hey," Connor said, "did I hear Mom was back?"

Steve O'Reilly was surprised by his son's question. "What?"

"I remember her saying she was here, back home."

Steve O'Reilly studied his son for a moment, then took a small chair by the wall and sat down next to Connor's bed.

"Connor," he said, "I don't know what you're thinking of. But you need to know that an unstable person—somebody who maybe doesn't really have control over what they say or do—someone like that can hurt you. They hurt other people all the time, and they hurt themselves when they do it. It's like they can't even help it. Well, I'm talking about your mom. She did wrong things to both of us. I'm still aching from that. I know you are."

Before he continued, he scooted the chair a little closer, leaned in.

"But listen to me. You can't let something like that keep you from loving somebody who you should love."

"What do you mean?" Connor asked. "Is she not coming back?"

"I don't know that I'd have her if she did, Connor. But I will say this: I am not going to sit around the rest of my life feeling sorry for myself. Last night, when I was certain I'd lost you, I cried—hard. And I thought how short all of our time is. I thought of many things I have regrets about, but my biggest regret was that I hadn't talked to you enough about going and doing what you love and trusting people ... well, trusting women."

Connor felt uneasy. He obviously had hallucinated hearing his mom's voice when he was in the Gulf.

"You get what I'm saying to you, Connor?" his dad asked.

"So Mom's not back?"

"No. But that's not what I'm saying. I'm saying that you shouldn't be afraid to love."

A floor nurse knocked on the door and poked her head in. Connor and his dad looked over at her.

"Sorry to intrude," she said. "There's somebody here asking to see Connor. You good with that?"

Connor thought about how he was going to react to Stamford coming in and apologizing for leaving him stranded in the Gulf overnight. At first he thought of fucking with him, but then he took a deep breath and decided to let Stamford know right away he wasn't going to blame one of his best friends for spending the night in the Gulf of Mexico.

"Sure," Connor said. "Send him in."

But it was Kassie who the nurse ushered into the room instead.

Connor was stunned into silence.

"Well," Connor's dad said, "let me guess. You're Kassie?"

"Yes sir," she said, nervously fumbling a bouquet of flowers and box of chocolates she had just bought down in the gift shop. *Thank God for small miracles and telephones,* Kassie thought. She had called the surf shop from a gas station in Sinton, and Sandi had answered.

"He's at Spohn," she'd told Kassie.

Steve O'Reilly turned around to Connor, leaned into his ear, and whispered: "I love you from here to the moon and back."

Then he stood and walked over to Kassie.

"Thanks so much for coming. I know it means a lot to my son. I was just going out for some coffee. Maybe you'd like something?"

"Oh, no, thank you, sir. I'm fine," Kassie said.

"All right, then," Connor's dad said. "I'll leave you two for a bit."

Kassie watched Steve O'Reilly leave before turning

around to face Connor. To him, she looked desperate, relieved, exhausted, uncertain—and absolutely beautiful.

"So," Connor said, "do you talk first, do I—whoa!"

Before Connor had time to finish his thought, Kassie had rushed forward, set the flowers and chocolates on the table, leaned over the bed rail, and was crushing him with a hug.

FORTY

KASSIE CLOSED the door of her family's condo and hurried down the steps. When she'd called home her mom and dad had been overjoyed to hear that Connor had been rescued. Her excitement bubbled over inside, making her feel like she was nervous, even though she wasn't. In fact, she had a growing confidence about her future and how it was going to look. They had talked about it and agreed while she was still in Connor's hospital room.

She hopped into her dad's Corvair and fired it up.

The drive to Gulf Beach Cottages from the Sea Isle condominiums took all of three minutes. The closer she got the tighter her body felt.

Kassie had spent that night in her family's condo alone. Port A was desolate in the offseason, so her parents didn't rent it out. It had been impossible to sleep, especially because Connor was so close by, but they had talked things through and decided that he needed to be with his dad that evening. She would come get him around lunchtime the next day, so she had hatched a plan in the meantime.

Cumulous clouds and low scud obscured the sun as she drove. Out in the Gulf, it looked like storms were brewing.

She thought about Perfect Saturday as she turned the corner at Eleventh and Avenue G, then saw Connor standing at Gulf Beach Cottages, waiting for her.

She pulled into the drive, then hopped out of the car and right into his arms, hugging him tight.

She pulled away, smiling at him.

"Long time no see, beautiful."

Connor smelled her freshly showered scent as he pressed his face into her lovely brown hair.

"Guess what I thought about all night long," he whispered.

"Maybe you can show me?"

"I wanted to be right there with you," Connor said. "But I'm glad I spent last night talking with Dad. We stayed up real late and had some good talk."

"I like that," she said. "Even so, that condo was pretty sad and empty last night, what with me being all alone and everything."

"Should we go cheer it up right now?"

Kassie wanted to say yes, yes let's go right now, but she didn't.

"First a quick surprise," she said. "Come on, get in the car."

Kassie pulled out onto Avenue G, drove a block, then turned right onto Station Street.

"Station Street," Kassie said. "Coast Guard station?"

"Coast Guard station," Connor replied. They held that thought for a minute. Then Connor turned to her with a question, jerked his thumb back over his shoulder, raised his eyebrows.

"Where are we going? Condo's the other way."

"You'll get your comeuppance soon enough," she said.

While she was busy driving, Connor watched all of Kassie's muscles moving: her thighs, her arms, even the way she moved her head to check for traffic at the stop signs. It made him so happy to watch her, when just two nights ago he thought he'd never see her again. Everything she did was beautiful, and her muscles looked amazing from the years of surfing she'd done.

Kassie revved the Corvair between upshifts, smiling at him. They passed by Connor's middle school, and it reminded him of how he and Franklin snuck away to the school library every chance they got to ogle the only surfing book on the shelves. It seemed like they had memorized every surf spot featured in *Modern Surfing Around the World*, which was ancient, having been published in 1964. Not surprisingly, Port Aransas wasn't one of the spots mentioned.

"Connor," Kassie said, softly, as they rounded a dogleg bend in the road, "that drive down here the other night was terrible, but I'd look at the sky and I'd imagine you swimming and keeping your eye on Polaris. I prayed that there would be no clouds so you could see it. I knew if you could see that star, you'd swim toward the beach. I wouldn't let myself believe you were gone."

"I did have my eyes on Polaris, and thank God the sky was clear," he said. "I backstroked westward all night long. Maybe your prayers worked."

As they pulled up to the intersection with Beach Street, Connor was momentarily confused by a crowd at Geri's Surfboard Shop.

"What the hell?" he said.

Kassie laughed.

"Yeah, what the hell," she repeated. Then she pulled

through the intersection and straight into the surf shop's parking lot.

Hung between two porch posts over the entrance was a banner that read:

Welcome Home!

Before he could move, a crowd of his friends and acquaintances surged forward, hooting and clapping.

"Go on, hop out," Kassie said.

Connor got out and was swarmed.

All of Connor's buddies came forward, shaking his hand and patting him on the back—someone shoved a cold Lone Star into his hand and told him to drink up.

"Slam that Lone Star down!" Robinson shouted.

Connor looked around with a big smile on his face.

"I don't know what to say," he said.

"Don't say," someone answered. "Swig!"

Connor raised the Lone Star bottle and started glugging.

"Go! Go! Go! Go!" the crowd shouted in unison.

As the fizzy beverage expanded in his mouth and throat, Connor thought he would spew a reverse chug before he finished but he managed to get it all in. Then—before he lowered the bottle—the skull-splitting crack from an ice cream headache struck.

He gave the empty bottle to Robinson and grabbed his head with both hands, hunched over.

"Argh!" he yelled. "Ice cream headache!"

The crowd hooted and laughed.

When he recovered, with Kassie standing at his side holding his hand, his friends and even a bunch of the surfers who normally ignored him came up to tell him they were glad he'd been rescued. They asked him how he had done it.

They were awed by his backstroke idea. Kassie got plenty of attention herself but kept firmly at Connor's side. She wanted everyone there to know beyond any doubt who she was with.

After everyone had welcomed him back the crowd began to break up into smaller groups. A few guys had set up a makeshift skateboard ramp on the Beach Street side of Geri's, on the parking lot of Boxcar Billy's. They were using a Super 8 millimeter camera to film each other skating, their skateboard wheels clacking as they spun off-the-lips over the top edge of the plywood ramp.

"Hey, isn't that Stamford over there?" Kassie asked, nudging Connor.

Connor saw Stamford hanging by the skateboard ramp. He wore his tatty blue OP corduroy shorts, flip-flops, a flowered shirt, sunglasses, and Connor's Denver Broncos baseball cap. He saw them looking at him and walked over.

Kassie tensed.

"Don't worry," Connor said, squeezing her hand. "We kissed and made up. Yesterday he dropped by with a six-pack of Lone Star. He offered me either the six-pack or to let me kick his ass. I chose the six-pack."

"Well, lookee here," Stamford said, smiling. "The hottest new couple on the island."

"Eh. Leave 'em alone, Stamford," Robinson said. "I oughta kick your ass."

"It wasn't his fault," Connor said. "Everybody needs to know that."

Stamford took off the Broncos cap and held it out to Connor.

"I think this is yours."

Connor smiled and took it.

"Thanks, bro. Now listen: Even though my adventure

wasn't due to you screwing up, I still have to give you notice. I'm not crew boating anymore."

"So I figured," Stamford said. "Maybe you could say a few kind words to my boss about what happened so I don't get shitcanned."

"So you don't get shitcanned?" Maxim said as he walked up from behind. He'd come out of the shop wearing nothing but his trademark loose-fitting white linen pants and a puka shell necklace. As ever, he was as ripped and as godly as Poseidon himself.

"Connor, dude!" Maxim said. "I was seriously worried about you. I was organizing a whole flotilla of fishing boats to go out looking for ya!"

He then came right up to Connor and gave him a huge bear hug.

"Ow. Hey!" Connor said, laughing, as Maxim lifted him off the ground, spun once, then set him down.

"No shit, man, we thought we'd lost you. I was rampaging mad at Stamford, but you got saved. Otherwise there might have been some real *violencia*."

Stamford frowned.

"And Kassie," Maxim said as he nodded at her, being extra polite, "glad to see you back. So, what's next?"

"Well, Kassie is headed out to Cali for a visit before she goes to college there," Connor replied.

"Where at?"

"San Diego," Kassie answered.

"Whoa! You're shitting me," Maxim said. "You're going to Cali and are gonna be riding all the good stuff while we suck down the washing-machine slop here in Texas."

"Black's, Windansea, La Jolla—all that," Kassie said.

Maxim then turned to look at Connor.

"What about you?" he asked.

Kassie put her hand on Connor's bicep to emphasize the next bit of news: "Don't worry, Maxim, *we'll* send you plenty of postcards!"

"Yeah," Connor added. " 'Wish you were here!' "

Maxim stood a little taller when he realized what Kassie meant. He nodded with approval at Connor.

"Well, well. So you agree, my brother," he said, gesturing leisurely at Kassie. "That right there is what it's all about."

Connor put his arm around Kassie.

"That's right, Maxim. This woman here, she's what *I'm* all about."

Maxim acted right pleased with himself. Then he turned and looked squarely at Stamford.

"And just think about it, y'all," he said, his voice turning aggressive. "You could've missed out on it because of this joker right here."

"Whoa, Maxim," Connor said, speaking up. "Me and Stamford, we're good. He didn't do anything wrong."

Maxim kept his eyes on Stamford but raised his hand back at Connor, like he was telling him to hush. Stamford had anticipated trouble, and he began glowering at Maxim. He puffed up and spoke: "You're just pissed because I've got a hundred bucks in my pocket that used to belong to you—or maybe the surf shop."

"Hey, let's not get ugly," Maxim said. "It was a friendly bet, and I lost. And for sure with my own money. At least I paid up, unlike you when you lose a bet, you fuck. I didn't leave my buddy stranded out in the Gulf and come all the way back into harbor before I figured it out."

"Me and Connor are cool on that," Stamford said. "I didn't do anything wrong."

"You're reckless," Maxim said. "You don't give a shit about anybody but yourself. Connor here deserves to be treated better. You know it, I know it, and everyone here knows it."

The people, in smaller and larger clumps, stopped their chit-chat to listen. As the discussion turned combative, the skaters stopped skating, and everyone in the parking lot was listening intently to the hard words Maxim was laying down.

"Take it easy, Maxim," Franklin said. "They talked it through."

"Bullshit," Maxim said, stepping a bit closer to Stamford. "I don't quite figure how you manage to get laid so often as you claim. You're probably lying about that."

Stamford stared hard at Maxim, turning red in the face, looking like he was about to pop. If this were at night, and if he'd been drinking ...

"Why don't you just chill, man," Stamford said. "Connor says it wasn't my fault. And it wasn't. I was just as worried about him as everyone else. I was sick over it."

"No, man," Maxim answered. "Here's the deal: You left Connor in the Gulf, and that wasn't the only time you did something like that. What about that time when you almost got Chris Kimble killed?"

"Dude, that was a freak accident," Stamford said, taken by surprise.

"No accident," Maxim said. "You took a guy who had never gone diving before to the rigs. No certificate, no training, nothing. The current swept him away from the rig and it took you guys like an hour to find him. He almost went under. Sounds familiar, don't it, guys?"

Maxim nodded his head and looked around at everyone, then pointed at Stamford, who looked like he was trying really hard to maintain his composure.

"Hey man, that was an accident, all right?" Stamford said. "Why you gotta bring that up?"

"One other thing," Maxim said, ignoring Stamford's question. "I know you were putting your hands all over Sandi's ass at Boxcar Billy's the other night. So watch it."

There was only so much public humiliation Stamford could take. Maxim knew it, and this last revelation to the crowd at the surf shop pushed Stamford over the edge.

"Sandi?" Stamford asked incredulously. "Why the hell would I put my hand on that little *puta's* ass?"

Instantly, Maxim crouched to strike, Stamford backed up as he raised his fists to block whatever was coming—and suddenly Kassie was standing between them.

"Stop!" she yelled. "Just fucking stop this nonsense!"

She held both arms out, the flat of one palm pointed at Maxim, the other at Stamford, like a traffic cop. But she spoke straight to Maxim.

"Let's just stand down," she said. "Forgive and forget. Stamford and Connor are good, and it was a freak accident. So just stand down, Maxim. I don't want my last day on the island—my surprise party for Connor—ruined by this bullshit."

No one spoke. Maxim looked kind of shocked, while Stamford stood behind Kassie, fists at the ready.

"Whatever you two need to solve, just wait until Connor and I leave," she said. "Do you think you can do that for me?"

Everyone stared at Maxim, who suddenly realized that all eyes were on him—and some of those eyes were filled with contempt. He eased out of his kung fu crouch, looking vaguely embarrassed.

"You're right, Kassie," he said quietly. Then he cast a look at Stamford, nodded apologetically, and sauntered slowly toward the surf shop's entrance.

Sandi came out of the shop and chided him: "Damn it, Maxim! Knock that shit off! It's bad for business."

Maxim casually walked up to the door Sandi was holding open for him, as though all was forgotten. He turned and waved at Connor and Kassie.

"Y'all have fun," he said. "Someday me and Sandi will come visit. In the meantime, catch some good waves—and send some good vibes our way!"

Then he disappeared inside the surf shop.

Stamford relaxed, gazing briefly at the door that had closed behind Maxim. Then he turned to face Kassie.

"Well," he said, "I owe you one, darlin'."

Connor wanted to laugh—but after looking at Kassie's tight-lipped expression, he knew he'd better not.

FORTY-ONE

THE CELEBRATION of Connor's rescue continued until the galvanized livestock watering tub had no more beer or wine coolers left in it. The partiers drifted off, one car at a time, and Connor's close buddies insisted on taking him and Kassie to eat at the Island Café. Connor got his usual: a cheeseburger and fries with a Dr Pepper. Afterward, Franklin and Robinson refused to let him pay.

"Eh, it's the least I can do for ya," said Robinson, who stayed Connor's hand as he tried to put down some dollars.

They went outside. It was late afternoon, and everyone had a little bit of a buzz from the surf shop party. Robinson gestured toward the sky, saying: "Thunderstorm's brewing up. Look how dark it is out over the Gulf. I think I'll go check the waves. Y'all want to go surfing?"

"Actually, we're going to go back over to Connor's place so he can hang out with his dad some," Kassie replied.

Connor looked at her, surprised. She squeezed his hand, smiling, before cocking her head a little.

"Right, Connor?" she asked.

"Right," he replied.

Robinson looked disappointed.

Connor was glad Kassie had shut down whatever was going through Robinson's mind. Maybe he still had eyes for Kassie—hell, everyone did—but that didn't matter to him anymore.

Connor and Kassie got into the Corvair, while Franklin and Robinson climbed into Franklin's white mail jeep, then slid the doors closed and drove off, surfboards strapped to racks across the top. They were headed down to the pier to check the waves.

Kassie turned to Connor.

"Let's go for a ride," she said.

"To the condo?"

"You'll see."

Kassie drove down the Island Road until they got to Beach Access Road No. 1, which took them down to the Gulf. It was smooth packed sand, completely empty. The water was glassy, dark green, and the sun was beginning its long, slow descent to the west. Out at sea the sky was dark gray.

At the horizon they saw a lightning bolt strike the water.

"Think any of your buddies will show up down here?" she asked.

"No," Connor said.

"I'm gonna put the top up, in case it rains," she said. "Then let's go for a walk."

They walked hand in hand along the deserted shoreline, watching the sandpipers scrambling at waters edge. Seagulls and pelicans flew past. A hundred yards out, a bottlenose dolphin came up for air, showing its dorsal fin for a moment, then submerged into the glassy, dark-green water.

It was getting dark. Billowing cumulous clouds moved

over them quickly, their tops reaching unknown heights—a preliminary show for the approaching thunderheads. The clouds above moved fast, but there was no wind on the beach. Out over the Gulf, they couldn't see where the sea ended and the sky began. It was just a solid pane of dark gray.

"This is a good spot," Kassie said. "Let's sit for a few minutes."

They sat down next to each other, watching the squalls in the Gulf. A few lightning bolts split the sky as the storm moved rapidly toward them. Connor looked at the skin on Kassie's thigh, then scooted closer so his leg touched hers. She put her warm hand into his, stared out to sea. They saw the rainfall getting closer.

"We're gonna get wet," Connor said.

"That's what I want," she answered.

Connor looked at her dark-brown legs, then put his hand gently on the top of her right thigh. Goosebumps rose up on Kassie's skin in response.

"You have the most beautiful skin on the whole planet," Connor said. "I'm sorry if it sounds like a cliché, Kassie, but you're the most beautiful woman I've ever known."

Kassie looked down at her legs. To her, they seemed different now than they did the night when she was upset and talking to her mom. Now they weren't just legs, and their purpose was clear: They needed to be wrapped around Connor's body, holding him tight against her.

A sudden cold gust of wind blasted down from the sky, strong enough to make them gasp. It lifted Kassie's hair, tossed it wildly. A lightning bolt burst nearby and thunder cracked the sky. They flinched and felt the concussion.

"Dang," Kassie said. "It's getting a little scary. But I don't want to leave."

Her free arm waved out at the Gulf's silvery waters, at

the small one-foot waves washing in and breaking at the shoreline, as raindrops started falling. They were fat drops, just a few at first, bringing that mysterious but vivid smell of rain. Kassie shivered at their cold impact; goosebumps rose on Connor's arms.

"Look," he said as they appeared, pointing and laughing. "I think I need to get warm."

Connor got up and moved behind her, then sat down so his body was pressed against hers, with his legs stretched around her. For Kassie, it felt good having him envelope her like he was—definitely heading in the right direction—but it wasn't quite enough.

The thunderstorm that had been a squall out in the Gulf a few minutes before now towered above them, and Connor's hands felt Kassie's chest as it rose and fell with her breathing.

The wall of gray they had seen as a haze in a distance was coming close enough to see that pulses of rain were swirling over the waters in random patterns, here harder and there lighter. It swept up, faster and faster, and they could hear the raindrops coming as a rush, the sound growing louder.

"It's almost here," Connor said.

The sheet of rain washed hard across the glassy nearshore water, then swept over them. Kassie screeched, and they were instantly soaked.

She leaned her head back, feeling Connor's warm lips on her neck, reached around with one hand and pulled her long brown hair out of his way so he could kiss more skin—her ear, her cheek—as the rain pounded down. He put his hands firmly on her breasts, kissed harder, she felt herself swelling, felt him swelling; she turned her face toward the heavens as she shuddered, the rain pummeling them with stinging drops, running in rivulets over their bodies and off onto the sand. Their clothes stuck to their skin. Connor's hands roamed all over her, and she parted her lips to taste the rain falling from the sky.

"Oh, my God," Kassie said when his hand rubbed between her thighs. "Connor, yes. Right now."

She twisted around, on her knees, her mouth on his—pressing, tasting him—when lightning struck so close that the thunderclap knocked them over. Kassie lay on top of him, laughing, undulating, when another explosion of lightning split the sky. It was a strobe of white, brighter than any Coast Guard searchlight. Thunder concussed their bodies and ears, they flinched with terror.

"Jeez," Connor said. "Let's get the hell out of here!"

Kassie whooped and they pulled each other up.

"Run," Kassie yelled.

They ran along the beach toward the car, stopping every few yards to kiss and feel one another, until another lightning bolt exploded nearby and made them run again. When they reached the Corvair they jumped inside, soaking wet, their hands on each other, pulling at clothes, kissing, shivering.

Suddenly, Kassie stopped.

"No," she said.

"What?" Connor asked, eyes growing wide.

"We're going to the condo, that's what," she said.

Kassie drove the Corvair back up the access road and straight to Sea Isle. The gray rain was coming down so hard that the Corvair's top had water leaking through some of the seams. They could barely see the road in front of them. Lightning kept striking close by. Connor thought how lucky he'd been. If this storm had happened that night he'd been lost at sea, he wouldn't be in this car right now.

FORTY-TWO

THEY DROVE to the condo in silence.

The storm had begun to abate when Kassie turned onto Sea Isle's curving driveway. Connor recalled the last time he'd driven on it, and how absurd his behavior had been.

She parked in front of her unit, the only car in the lot.

They got out and started up the stairs, Kassie leading him by the hand.

The sky over the Gulf was a monotone curtain of dark gray but the sun glinted in the west, peaking out below the bottoms of the storm clouds.

"Oh, my God," said Kassie, who stopped cold when they got to the balcony of her floor.

She pointed toward the Gulf.

"Look."

Stretched across the dark sky over the wide Gulf was a lucid double rainbow arcing a hundred and eighty degrees over the silvery waters.

"I've never seen anything like that, Connor. Have you?"

"No," he replied.

"That's real beauty," said Kassie. "I've got nothing on it. Nothing at all."

She unlocked the door, and they went in; she closed the door behind. They stood there at the entrance in the chilly air-conditioned condo shivering, water dripping from their bodies and clothes.

Kassie stepped out of her flip-flops, flicking them aside with her foot. Connor did the same.

"So you've got nothing on the beauty of that rainbow out there?" he asked.

"No."

"Let's find out, Kassie."

His hands ran slowly down over her torso, pressed her wet blouse against her body. His fingers clasped onto the hem at the bottom, then slowly pulled the bottom of her blouse up so that the wet fabric peeled away from her skin. She kept gazing up at him, raised her arms so he could pull it over her head.

He dropped it on the floor.

Kassie shivered.

"Are you cold?" he asked.

"I think it's a little unfair of you to take my blouse off while you keep your T-shirt on."

She put her fingers on the hem of Connor's T-shirt and pulled it up. He also lifted his arms, and she got it over his head, letting it drop with a wet slap onto the floor next to her blouse.

Outside another shower of rain swept in, pelting the windows, the balcony, the closed door. They heard the water splashing down a roof gutter drain—a distant thunderclap rumbled. Kassie leaned forward and put her lips on Connor's pectoral muscle, tasting salt and rainwater, put her hands on his hips. When she looked up toward his face, she saw rivulets of water from his soaked hair dripping down over his shoulders.

"It seems unfair," Connor said as he pointedly looked down at her black bikini top cupping her breasts. "We can't have me topless if you're not."

From her breast, he ran his finger under the strap of her bikini top, up over her shoulder, and then down to where it joined the back strap. He reached around with his other hand, tracing the back strap softly until both hands met in the middle of her back. Kassie's back arched involuntarily at the light pressure, and her breasts pushed into Connor; his fingers effortlessly untied the knot of string.

They pulled apart, both looking down to see.

Connor pulled the bikini top away from her. It peeled off her breasts and made her catch her breath. He let the top fall to the floor, where it landed on the small heap of wet clothing.

She felt herself swell. Connor was hardening, straining against his Birdwells.

"Only a bit more to remove," she said, looking down at it.

She moved over it and around it with her hand, its heat provoked an ache inside her cleft, demanding immediate relief. She casually untied his board shorts, then used her thumbs to slide them down over his hips. Leaning down a little, she pushed them down toward his knees, and they fell the rest of the way to the floor on their own.

His hardness snapped out and bumped against her breasts. She lingered, but a moment, then kissed him there. Then she slowly stood.

"Only one thing left," she said, placing his hands on either side of her hips.

He looked down at her shorts and started to roll them off her body, including her black bikini bottoms. Kassie let him take his time. She felt his breath on her shoulder; she kissed his exposed neck.

The bikini bottom flopped to the floor and she stepped out of it.

Now there was nothing but the two of them.

All my life, Connor thought. *This girl. How had this happened?* There was no doubt in his mind that she was the other part of him that had been the ache, that hole left inside by a trauma caused by someone else. Now he had to hand himself to Kassie.

He saw her tremble.

"I'm not cold," she said. "It's you making me shake like this."

One soft embrace, a kiss—then Kassie led him out of the kitchen, over the carpeting of the living room, through the short hall, and straight to her bedroom.

"Now," she said, and got up on the bed on her knees, facing him. He stood on the floor in front of her. His stiffness poked at her belly, her hand automatically reached down to it. Then they were kissing like they really meant it.

"I said *now,*" she repeated, then slowly lay back on the bed. Connor took in her beauty in that moment—everything she was right now, everything she had ever been before, and everything she would be in times to come.

He got up onto the bed, aligned himself with her, his arms keeping him just slightly above.

Kassie reached down and stroked him.

"I like it," she whispered.

She lifted her hips up, delirious with desire. Connor saw her brown eyes widen. He lowered himself down so his body touched lightly against hers from hips to chest. He felt her warm breath on his neck, smelled that familiar hint of Yves Saint Laurent perfume she used so deftly.

Kassie felt only pleasure in his body pressing against hers, with no doubts at all in her mind. It seemed to her that this moment was all that ever needed to be. She calmed down completely, stopped shivering. Above her was all she craved: raw desire, pure confidence, and devotion. The two of them together in this moment rivaled the beauty of a bright double rainbow under the Gulf Coast sun. She parted her legs.

"So, I'm yours?" he asked.

"Yes," she said. "You're mine."

EPILOGUE

CONNOR STOOD at the crest of the bluff, looking down at the blue Pacific, still amazed that he was now regularly surfing waves at Black's, a surf spot he'd ogled for years in the pages of *Surfer* and *Surfing* magazines. No more dreaming: He was looking in person at long lines of lined-up, clean waves that moved slowly from the deep water to the littoral before they peaked and broke hard on the suddenly shallow sandbars.

He heard light footsteps coming up behind, knew exactly who he would see when he turned to look.

"Hi," Kassie said, eyes bright, a smile on her face as though she were meeting him for the first time ever and wanted him to like what he saw.

"Hi," he answered back.

Kassie peered past him over the edge and tiptoed, her tight wetsuit outlining every beautiful curve of her body, her hair tossed by the breeze.

"Damn, it looks good down there today."

"Six foot?" Connor asked.

"At least," she said.

Connor watched as a small dark figure of a surfer paddled into an overhead wave and dropped in, making a good bottom turn but getting wiped out by a section that broke in front and enveloped the surfer in a wall of whitewater.

"Too deep," they said, simultaneously.

Kassie laughed.

She came right up to Connor and stretched up to kiss him.

"It's like our brains are connected," she said.

"They are," he said.

"Good day to skip class, huh?"

"You probably shouldn't," he said, "seeing as how you've got a midterm tomorrow."

"If I don't know the mechanics of heat-shield ablation by now, I'm doomed anyway," she said. "I need to *surf*."

Then she looked up at him, raising her eyebrows like her mom.

"And you?" she asked him. "What's your excuse?"

"Large mammal marine biology can do without Connor O'Reilly for the afternoon, don't you think? Besides, I thought it would be a good idea to make some up-close and personal scientific observations."

Connor pointed down at the beautiful waters of Black's Beach, where they often came to escape, sometimes even during scheduled classes.

"See that?" he asked.

Kassie peered down at the water, searching.

"What is it?" she asked.

"There. See them?"

In that moment, Kassie saw four bottlenose dolphins racing through the water inside a large wave.

"Oh, my God," she exclaimed.

There were two adults and two juveniles. As the wave walled up steeper, they burst through the face and sailed through the air, then arced down to the bottom of the wave and plunged back into the water. They did it again and again before the wave finally broke, then they went deep out of sight, only to reappear outside the lineup to do it again.

Connor was transfixed watching the dolphin family at play. When he came to, he realized that Kassie had reached out and was holding his hand. She looked up at him and was smiling. The afternoon sun glinted in her brown eyes.

"So, like them?" she asked.

Connor smiled at her.

"Yeah," he said. "Just like them."

The End

ABOUT THE AUTHOR

Skip Rhudy grew up surfing in Port Aransas, Texas.

He has translated poetry and prose from the German and translated Wolfgang Hilbig's novella *Die Weiber* for his master's thesis in 1990 at UT Austin. His short stories were published in numerous small press magazines in the mid 1990s, and his novella *One Punk Summer* was published in 1993 and reprinted in 2021.

Skip works as a software developer. He holds a patent in TCP/IP acceleration, and is building an airplane. He and his wife live in Tulsa, Oklahoma, have two daughters, three dogs, and a horse named Pierre.

Looking for your next book?
We publish the stories you've been waiting to read!

Scan the QR code below to get 20% off your next Stoney Creek title!

For author book signings, speaking engagements, or other events, please contact us at info@stoneycreekpublishing.com

StoneyCreekPublishing.com

www.ingramcontent.com/pod-product-compliance
Lightning Source LLC
LaVergne TN
LVHW020032120325
805460LV00004B/15